SUNRISE AT AN LAC

Alex Rushton

For Astrid, Carl, Josh, Nyle and Freya,
Enjoy!..
with best wishes
Alex Rushton
X

SCRIPTORA

September '14

Published in Great Britain 2014 by

SCRIPTORA

25 Summerhill Road

London N15 4HF

in association with SWWJ (The Society of Women

Writers & Journalists)

scriptora.publ@btinternet.com

This is a work of fiction. Any resemblance between the
fictional characters and actual persons, living or dead, is
coincidental.

ISBN 978-0-9562494-7-0

Printed and bound by Witley Press Hunstanton PE36 6AD

For Trevor
Without whom this book would not have been written.

Many thanks to my editor, Mary Rensten.

Thanks also to John and Pat Jones, Shelley Miller, Guy Blythman, Wendy Hughes and Angela Horne for their support and comments on earlier versions of this manuscript.

CHAPTER 1

May 2033

An Lac ashram, Switzerland

Ralph stood in front of the photograph of the planet earth taken from space, one of the few unnecessary objects in the whole ashram. Whenever he looked at it he felt humbled; the sphere looked so fragile hanging there in that vast cosmic arena. He thought of the arrogance of previous generations who ignored the warnings, raped the planet and left their deadly legacy. His small effort now seemed insignificant in the whole scheme of things, but at the same time he knew it wasn't. He remembered Ajahn Annando saying long ago that you needed to change the colour of only one tile to change a whole mosaic. He felt a rush of cool air on his sleeveless arms and his face. Turning he saw a curtain puffed out at an open window; it sucked back suddenly and puffed out again beating to and fro against the wall. Ralph went to the window and looked out; a freshening wind thrashed the branches of the trees and blew the raindrops horizontal. Below, sun patches skidded across the grassy valley. Towards the mountains far away the trees in the pine wood shifted restlessly. He turned as the other four came in; the wooden chairs screeched as they pulled them into position around the circular pine table. Ralph shivered. The window boomed as he shut it and the caught wind died out of the room. Ralph took his seat, across from the others. Looking at Ajit, Ralph noticed for the first time a few white hairs in Ajit's goatee beard. We're all getting older, he reflected. Although Erin looked more like a twenty-something than the thirty-something he knew her to be.

1

'This shouldn't take long,' he said, 'then we can get back to our usual tasks. Maurice, would you start. What's the latest situation with the communications? Just a summary please.'

Maurice ran his fingers through his greying afro hair. 'I've got some difficulty communicating with several parts of Europe at the moment. Particularly northern Italy, France and also Spain.'

'That's where Imam Ali is in charge, isn't it?' Erin spoke briskly. 'I've heard bad things about him.'

'He's strong and he rules the area with a rod of iron. That's well known,' Maurice said.

Erin sat back and crossed her arms. 'We can't know for sure but I guess refugees are still swarming across the Med. into Spain?'

'They were two months ago.'

'If we're going to be effective we really need clear detailed information,' said Erin.

Maurice straightened up. 'Look. It's really difficult; I can never get the whole picture. Western Europe is in chaos, the provision of resources is patchy. From what I can tell, in some places agriculture and manufacturing are continuing in some form or other. In others people are improvising and small groups have become self-sufficient. Some countries like Belgium have become isolationist and closed their borders. As you know several have had a breakdown in law and order and civic infrastructure. And it's changing all the time, it's like chasing a moving target.'

'Look, we know you're doing your best,' Ralph smiled at him encouragingly.

Ralph sensed the atmosphere in the room was abnormally tense. He noticed Isabella sitting stiffly on the edge of her seat. Her blonde hair wasn't pinned into a tight bun as usual but hung loose over the shoulders of her long white dress; unusually she wasn't wearing a slip and he could see the outline of her bra. Ralph looked away quickly.

'Are you able to communicate with Eastern Europe?' said Ajit quietly.

Ralph was pleased Ajit had joined the conversation. His soothing Indian accent always had a calming effect on everyone.

Maurice cleared his throat. 'Yes. In the East the picture's clearer. The New Islamists have a stranglehold there as well but I can tell you that there are dozens of our underground groups springing up in Greece, Romania and Slovakia in particular. Where our contacts are active they've been distributing leaflets and using spies to identify possible recruits, and it's working.'

'So Annando's message is getting out to the masses at last,' said Erin.

'What exactly is the message they're getting?' asked Ralph.

'Well, some of them have already heard of Annando and have been practising sustainability and self-reflective consciousness for years. They're spreading the message that this simple lifestyle he's promoting is good and the only way humanity can move forward. They've rejected secular materialism and its excesses and they're worried about being unwittingly drawn into the New Islamist order. They see Annando's simple way as the middle way between two extremes, the only valid alternative.'

'We're not just talking about intellectuals and people on the fringe, are we?' asked Ralph.

'No, I think it's getting through that this is for everybody, everywhere.'

'Are they operating in isolation?' Ralph asked.

'Where they are able to they are linking with other groups. The network is growing all the time. Some of the groups have been infiltrated by the New Islamists, but because they're small and mobile they are able to reform quickly. On the whole the feedback is good.'

Ralph noticed Isabella twirling her long ringlet around her finger and smoothing the creases in her dress. She had a strange, vacant expression.

'What about the UK, Norway and Sweden, north west Europe?' said Ajit.

'The picture is patchy. It's hard to get a complete grip on the situation. I need to do some more work to improve communications there. It's tricky keeping in touch with our contacts in the outside world without alerting our attackers to what we're up to. And also without giving away where we are.'

Ralph nodded. 'Yes, I know it can't be easy. Any sign of intruders on our network?'

'No. We have software constantly monitoring the integrity of our local network and as far as I can tell it has not been penetrated. There have been no intruder alerts and the honey pots remain untouched.'

'Honey pots?' said Erin. 'What are they?'

'They are groups of data that superficially look enticing. They have all sorts of interesting titbits in there: anyone snooping on our network would find them alluring, I hope. All made-up stuff, of course. If anyone from outside even browses them all sorts of silent alarms would be triggered and we would be able to monitor what they were up to. The idea is that once we detect someone looking at the honey pots they will find sufficient there to keep them on the system long enough for us to trace where they're coming in from and take countermeasures. With any luck though no-one will get in past our defences. Anyone got any questions?' Maurice looked at the others in turn.

'That's intriguing. I'd like to take a look at the system with you later if that's OK,' said Erin.

'Of course,' said Maurice, 'I could always do with some help.'

'I don't understand any of this,' said Isabella.

That's not true, thought Ralph, Isabella with her PhD in astrophysics, that's a strange thing for her to say and her voice sounds tense.

'Erin, you're the expert, you've been monitoring it. I want to know what's happening in the rest of the world,' said Isabella.

Ralph looked round the room, Ajit shrugged, Maurice shook his head.

'Yes, Erin, please give us an update,' said Ralph. 'There are some more natural disasters I suppose.'

'I'm afraid so, the situation continues to deteriorate. Overall the best guess of how many people worldwide have been displaced so far just by the rise in sea level is about 600 million.' Erin stood up and deftly pushed her hair behind her ears. She unrolled a world map, spread it on the table and secured the corners with paper weights. 'Some places are no longer reachable. Japan, for instance, has had a new spate of earthquakes – we've lost all contact there. Cairo has now gone. It's no longer on the Nile, it's under it.' As she talked she pointed to the locations and traced her finger back and forth along the coast lines. 'It's pretty much the same all over. Places that have been hanging on have now succumbed to the inevitable.' She stopped, took a deep breath, stood up straight and put her hands in the pockets of her denim jeans.

'What about Ian... Ian in Sydney?' said Isabella. Ralph heard her voice tremble.

Erin frowned. 'I haven't heard from Ian.'

Ralph looked around, everyone was still, Isabella sat stiff, frozen.

'And Sam, what does Sam say?' Isabella asked.

'Let's talk about this later, shall we?' said Ralph.

5

'That would be a good idea,' Ajit said gently.

'No, no, tell me the truth,' Isabella's voice became animated, 'Erin tell me. Sam was with him.'

Erin hesitated for a moment and frowned.

'Sam is now in Canberra. He says that Eastern Australia … around Sydney, has been hit by a tsunami and central Australia is a dustbowl.' Looking straight at Isabella in a soft voice she said, 'I'm sorry.'

Ralph saw the colour drain from Isabella's cheeks as she dropped her eyes and hid her face in her hands. Her chest heaved and he heard her heavy breathing almost like a death rattle. Ralph took a deep breath. Cool, analytical Isabella is losing the plot, he thought. When she pulled her hands away, her face was crumpled and ugly. The lines around her eyes made her look much older than her thirty seven years. Her small blue eyes were welling with tears. Ajit went to her and gently put his arm over her shoulder.

'No, Ajit!' She glared at him and savagely pushed him away. Ajit was thrown backwards; he stumbled and clung onto the table with one hand, his kurta pajama caught on the back of a chair. He released it and pulled himself upright. 'Tasks, that's all you think about, tasks. You've become hard. See yourselves.' As she sprang to her feet her golden hair whipped round her face, her cheeks suddenly flushed red. 'We used to start the meeting with words of appreciation and hopes for the day. All that's gone now. You run the meeting like… like a business… a military operation… see yourselves! Ralph, you're always tense, Maurice is like a walking computer, Erin a Nazi commander. Ajit, you're the only one who… Isn't anybody human anymore? And as for Annando, I can't think what would happen if any of you took over… no one else has his insight and wisdom. It's too terrible to bear!' Her chair screeched as she forced it aside. 'You're all rubbish,' she yelled and ran towards the door.

Briskly Ajit followed her.

'Go away, leave me alone!' she screamed.

Ajit stood still watching her go, and slunk back to his seat.

Ralph scratched his chin. 'I'm concerned about her. She hasn't been the same since Ian went missing.'

'They've always been close, twins often are,' said Maurice.

'And she hasn't been to meditation for three weeks,' said Ajit.

'I'm sorry. I should have been more sensitive.' Erin frowned. 'I've put my big foot in it. What a way to describe me. I've let her down; I've let you all down. I feel bad.'

'One person feeling bad is enough,' said Ralph, 'don't punish yourself. She had to find out sometime.'

'I will go to Isabella, later,' said Ajit.

Erin nodded. 'Yes, you are the best person.'

'Let's finish the meeting here, shall we?' said Ralph.

'I agree,' said Ajit.

'Wait,' Maurice held up his hand and looked at his communicator. 'There's a message coming through. It's about Carlos.'

Erin leaned forward. 'What does it say?'

'There's not much detail but it isn't good news. Apparently he's been arrested, in Madrid.' Maurice sighed, deeply.

'Do you know how it happened? Where is he?' said Ralph.

'Oh no, he only left here three months ago.' Erin frowned. 'Determined to run the network as effectively as I can he said. Now this.'

'Who's taken him and why?' said Ralph.

'Look, I've got a really poor line.' Maurice stroked his forehead. 'This came through the network of messengers, not the email route, sorry I've got very little information.

All I know is that it happened in Madrid and that's where he's being held.'

'What could Carlos have done?' said Erin, her voice loud and tense with frustration. 'Surely he's smart enough not to put himself in danger.'

'He can be passionate and wilful though, at times.'

'Yes, you're right, Maurice, he never was one for holding back, not your best diplomat,' said Ralph.

'It might not have been him, he might have been betrayed,' said Erin.

'Look, there's nothing we can do about it right now, not until we're better informed,' said Ralph.

Maurice looked up. 'I'll let you know as soon as I hear any more, OK?'

'Maybe I should go there myself,' said Erin.

Ralph leaned forwards. 'Don't be hasty, all in good time. Meanwhile, let's all get back to work.'

Ralph let them all leave the room first. He took the back route through the fire exit and onto the garden path; the gravel crunched under his shoes. The May midday sun was bright and the wind had softened to a gentle breeze. He undid the top button of his shirt and breathed in the fresh air, smelling the sweet perfume of the myrtle shrubs. After about a hundred metres the gravel petered out and the path became bare earth. It will be another long day, he thought. Many of the days are like this now, full of challenges and uncertainty, both in the ashram and beyond. Around him the birds sang in the bushes, he wondered for how much longer. In the distance the mountains stood, majestic and daunting. Some still had snowcaps; he wondered for how much longer they would be there too. Don't be negative; he said to himself, it's not helpful, not to me or anyone else. I must remain positive, whatever happens. 'Tense all the time,' Isabella's wrong about that.

He heard a faint whimpering from below and looked down towards the lake. On the path Isabella was enfolded in Tom's arms. Ralph gritted his teeth and his loose hands became tight fists. He stopped, took a few deep breaths and calmed himself. He'd give Tom the benefit of the doubt this time, that Tom was being helpful for once, and not just taking advantage, but Ralph was determined that this would be young Tom's last such chance.

CHAPTER 2

Ralph stepped inside and slammed the front door behind him. One more step and he was right in their small kitchen/dining room. There was a smell of burnt toast.

'What's the matter?' Jane stood at the sink with her hands in the washing up bowl. Her shabby ankle-length dress was splattered with water. As she spun round her long dark plait flicked behind her like a horse's tail. 'Well?'

'I saw Tom with his arms around Isabella!' He almost spat the words out. He lifted the pile of clean threadbare towels that lay haphazardly on the seat, put them on the floor and flung himself into the armchair.

'Maybe he was trying to comfort her; she hasn't been herself lately.'

'Comfort! He doesn't know what comfort is. She's nothing to him, like any other female member of the human race. He hasn't got a compassionate bone in his body.'

'So you think he's just trying it on?' She peeled off her rubber gloves and placed them over the edge of the sink. He saw her face once fresh and engaging now tired and lined with the imprint of drudgery and toil. 'She is over eighteen, in fact twice his age.'

'So what, she's vulnerable. I don't think she's trying to corrupt him.'

'Isabella has always been the epitome of purity to you hasn't she? You put her on a pedestal.'

Ralph heard the irritation in her voice; he'd heard it often lately. 'So you think it's OK for our son to come on to a Brahma Kumari do you?'

'Maybe he was just trying to comfort her... and if he wasn't, well...'

'I can't believe you're saying this. You don't care about Isabella's welfare then?'

'See it from Tom's point of view: he's young, she's a pretty woman and he likes the way she dances; she dances a lot.'

'Dances! The dance is an expression of her spirituality, for God's sake. Come on Jane, you know Tom. He'll translate anything into his own vocabulary of lechery. In Tom's eyes she may as well be lap dancing! The whirling dervishes, they dance and swirl ecstatically to the music. There's nothing remotely sexual about that, unless there's a female dancing and it's Tom watching. It's about how you interpret what you see, you see the world through your own blinkers and Tom's blinkers are lecherous.'

'Dancing can be erotic whether it's intended to be or not.'

'Only if you've got a corrupt mind.'

'Ralph, you've become such a prude.'

'I'm not prudish, I'm just trying to set some standards.'

'You expect too much from him. He's only a young man. In fact you expect too much from us all. You expect us to live by your *impossible* standards.' She looked at him scornfully. He sensed the bitterness concealed in her words. 'Take me for instance. First you refuse contraception and our family gets larger and larger and now, in order to purify yourself, or for whatever reason, you insist on being celibate. If you carry on like this you may as well put on the robes and go and live like Annando!'

The door burst open and Tom stood there, upright and confident, grinning, He reminded Ralph of his younger self, but Tom had a wilfulness Ralph had never had. Tom's sharp eyes scanned the room. Abruptly, Ralph stood up. Tom averted his gaze.

'Hi, Dad.'

'What were you doing with Isabella?'

'Nothing.'

11

Tom glanced at Ralph for less than a second but that was enough for Ralph to read the defiance and excitement in Tom's expression, his thrill of tasting the forbidden fruit. Tom started for the stairs.

'Leave Isabella alone; she's not herself. Look at me when I'm talking to you. Do you hear me?'

'We get on well, Dad.'

'You leave her alone.'

'She likes me. Shut up and mind your own business.' Tom zipped up the stairs.

'Don't talk to me like that,' called Ralph. Tom was out of sight.

'Well, you handled that well, didn't you,' said Jane. 'What's happened to your tact Ralph? Cool off. You make us all agitated.' Her voice snapped like a string that had been screwed up too tightly. 'What's happening to you?'

'Look, it's such a mess in here, why don't you let me tidy up.' He picked up a cloth, dampened it and wiped the crumbs from the table. Lifting the pile of towels from the floor he walked over and put them on the stairs. 'Here, they're ready to go upstairs now.'

'Stop it Ralph, you're just getting in the way with your cleaning; will you leave it alone.' Abruptly she got hold of the pile and put it back on the armchair. 'Stop trying to control us all... '

Ralph grimaced. Not that again, he thought. Once it started the argument went round and round like an old fashioned vinyl LP with the needle stuck in a groove, almost word for bitter word. She was still talking; he recognised the words and the tone of voice but mentally he'd switched off.

'Not now, Jane.' He took the few steps to the front door and slammed it behind him.

*

Ralph walked briskly along the gravel path between the simple houses and wooden clad bungalows neatly spaced out on the mountainside plateau. Their solar panels shone like mirrors in the sunlight. It's not right, he thought, she's my wife, I love her but I just want to get away from her. Is it her or is it me; what's gone so wrong? He stopped for a moment and let the strong breeze cool his hot body. Looking down towards the valley he saw the people from the community working in the fields and heard the buzz of the machinery in the dairy. Stefano, in his blue work overall, led a cow on a rope into the meadow. He smelt the milk, hot and fresh. A few children played noisily with skipping ropes outside the schoolhouse. After five minutes he had left the ashram and followed a path leading between thinly spaced lofty coniferous trees. The brown earth was covered sparsely with pine needles, cones and small patches of sunlight. His nostrils filled with the sharp tang of pine resin. He came to an opening with a view. On the other side of the valley a green wood clung like a parasite to the mountain. He sat down on a patch of earth, looked out, then took some moments in meditation. So much for solitude, he thought when he heard footsteps crunch on the gravel path.

'Ralph, I've been looking for you,' said Erin, 'Stefano said you'd come this way.' Wisps of brown hair blew around her face in the breeze; she pushed them behind her ears.

'What is it?'

'The electrical output from the main CHP unit, it's fluctuating again. I'd ask Isabella to sort it out as it's her responsibility but...'

'OK, I'll look at it, the wiring may need replacing.'

She sat down beside him. 'Ralph, what's up? You look very grim.'

Ralph sighed, 'Is it that obvious?'

'I've known you long enough.'

'I caught Tom with his arms around Isabella and I don't think he was trying to comfort her.' As he said it he felt himself bristle with irritation.

'Oh.' Erin frowned and looked at him intently. 'He's got a reputation, hasn't he? Isabella must be more sick than we thought.'

'Well, he's known for leading girls astray, but Isabella, can you imagine!'

Erin frowned. 'Yes I can imagine, sadly.'

'He's lived most of his life in this ashram where we've all shown him how to live with respect and consideration and he's turned out like this, despite it all.' Ralph sighed heavily. 'I don't know where I've gone wrong.'

'Maybe you haven't gone wrong. It's just him. After all he can be charming. He's got a real way with him.'

'He's an opportunist and she's vulnerable,' said Ralph.

'I agree she's vulnerable, but she's got lots of support from Annando and Ajit. Let it go, Ralph, you've got enough responsibilities as it is.'

Ralph sighed heavily again.

'Is there anything else that's wrong?' said Erin.

'Not really. Well Jane, if you must know.' He said her name dismally, as if it pained him. 'She says I'm too controlling. Maybe I do expect too much.'

'Maybe you expect too much of yourself as well. You can't be perfect, Ralph.'

'That's what we're all struggling to be isn't it, perfect, like Annando.'

'The difference is that we struggle to be perfect and Annando doesn't. Buddhist monk that he is, he doesn't need two hundred and twenty seven precepts. He's there, he lives the precepts automatically. Anyway, we shouldn't be struggling, we should be letting go.'

'You're right, of course we should,' said Ralph. 'How could I have forgotten that? Do you remember, only a few years ago the ashram was such a peaceful place, the daily routine worked like clockwork, we were one large harmonious family, any conflicts were quickly resolved. We were the ideal community, people flocked to us to live and learn.'

'And now we're in a secret hideout. The world is different now. The rate of change has been phenomenal. Who would even have guessed that natural disasters like this would have battered the earth and that all the political and industrial systems that we took for granted would come tumbling down? Even here in the ashram, we're not immune to all that.'

'Annando wouldn't want us to be immune anyway. He'd want us to read the signs of the times.'

'Read them, not get swept along with them. Maybe Isabella is right. Maybe we have all become too task orientated. I was insensitive in the meeting. Isabella said I was like a Nazi commander. That hurt me. I should have talked to her about Ian first. It was thoughtless of me.'

'We're all inadequate. Maybe that's why Annando doesn't want to choose any of us as his successor,' mused Ralph. 'We all have our faults, I've been told I'm too tense and controlling, you can come across as intimidating, Maurice is a complete geek, even Isabella is too ethereal sometimes.'

'Now you are being critical. That's your interpretation, not Annando's. Who knows why Annando makes the decisions he does, he's unfathomable. We question his decisions, then a few months later we realise he was right. How often has that happened?'

'Always. He only gets it wrong when he's given the wrong information, never when he uses his own insights or intuition or whatever else he uses.'

They sat in silence for a few moments.

'He seems to have a bird's eye view of the world, sees everything so clearly,' said Erin. 'Do you remember that story he tells us about the blind men and the elephant. That one blind man feels the elephant's leg and thinks it's a tree trunk, and another man feels its tail and thinks it's a rope...'

'And another feels the ear and thinks it's a fan.'

'Well, for me we're all like that, partially blind, only realising one bit of the whole thing, except for Annando, who has the insight to see it all.'

'That's why he's the guru.'

'And that's why we're all here.'

'But we didn't expect this, did we?' Ralph suddenly burst into a sharp abrupt laugh. 'None of us are experienced Field Marshals who've been promoted by our ability and experience to mastermind the world as a disaster zone.'

'The world as a disaster zone. It sounds so final,' said Erin dismally. 'There must have been other civilisations that burnt themselves out.'

'History is littered with them. They were sophisticated in their day but overstretched themselves.'

'Tell me.'

'The Sumerians, the Babylonians and the Easter Islanders are just three of them. Nobody knows what happened to the people who were there at the end. Perhaps they abandoned their homes and cities and went to more abundant pastures.'

'We don't have that choice though, do we? There's nowhere safe to go.'

'No, this time we may all be done for.'

Erin sighed, and looked out thoughtfully to the horizon. She sat up a bit straighter.

'Let's not be too dismal. The situation is very grave but there's still hope.'

'You think so?'

'Yes I do. You know how we do things here at An Lac. We always try to work with the environment, looking after it as it looks after us. Those other groups take their inspiration from us and from Annando's teachings. That's the way forward.'

Ralph held her gaze. 'We have the slight obstacle of the new order of fundamentalist imams who are out to destroy us and Islamise the world. Ten years ago we had no idea that one day we would be coordinating a worldwide resistance movement.'

'No, none of us could have foreseen this.'

'God, I hope we're up to the job.'

'Whatever the pressures, we mustn't lose our core values,' said Erin. 'I keep thinking about Carlos. We didn't know what he was going to did we.'

'No, but Carlos was bold, determined as ever.'

'The children miss him. I miss him.'

'We all do.'

Ralph sighed. 'Do me a favour will you? I wasn't good with Tom today, I overreacted, got angry. If you see me being controlling, tell me.'

'Surely it's better for you to ask Jane about that.'

Ralph said nothing and looked at Erin.

'Thank God I'm not married and never intend to be,' said Erin. 'That institution is for people braver than I. Yes, I'll tell you if you're impossible, and vice versa.'

Ralph stretched and stood up. 'Well, I'd better go and see to that unit.'

As they passed the dairy in the valley below Stefano waved to them. He had a chicken tucked under his arm. It squawked and wriggled.

'Stefano's happy, in his element, busying himself all day doing his regular jobs; he likes things always the same, hates change,' said Ralph.

'And resists taking on anything new.'

'But when he does it's always OK; I wish he'd more confidence in himself.'

'I've always thought he was wasted doing all these manual tasks but I suppose he's in his comfort zone. He's quite clever really; I love his poetry.'

Stefano walked towards them.

'He may not like it but change is coming; he'll have to face it soon enough, as we all will,' said Ralph. As he neared Stefano there was an earthy pungent smell.

'Hi, how are you?' said Ralph.

'I'm fine,' said Stefano. His eyes were clear and his smile lit up his face with brightness and warmth.

'All's well at the farm?' Ralph said.

'Yep, I'll put this girl back then I'm off to clean the chimney.'

'What would we do without you?' said Erin.

'Well you won't need to find out,' said Stefano confidently.

'Dirty job that,' said Ralph.

'I'm used to it,' said Stefano.

'See you later then.' Erin waved as Stefano walked away.

Ralph and Erin made their way back towards the main buildings.

CHAPTER 3

Madrid, Spain

'Right, so I'll need the essay by Monday.' Carlos projected his voice briskly and confidently across the classroom. 'This being Saturday that gives you the rest of today and also tomorrow to finish it. Use your notes from the last three lessons. Remember to explain what is meant by the terms tectonic plates, earthquakes and tsunamis. I'd like a recent example of each one and some detailed sketches with clear labels.' He lifted his arm, waved his three papers in the air and looked sharply about the room. 'Now has everyone got three pieces of lined paper?'

Thirty teenagers looked towards him with wide eyes and open expressions. 'Yes,' they said, almost in chorus.

'Don't be wasteful. This is all the paper I can spare and it'll help you to write carefully and succinctly. Bring any pieces back that you haven't used.'

Stelios raised his hand. 'Sir?'

'Yes, Stelios.'

'I heard that some of the tent city children might be coming to our school. Is that right?'

'It's only a rumour. There are no definite plans I know about.'

'But if there's not enough paper for us, then there won't be enough paper for them either.'

'Even children living in tents need an education,' said Carlos.

'Then we'd only have to write half an essay,' said Lourdes.

'I've heard that over in Germany they've got a paper factory still working and loads of paper but they won't let us have it because we're a poor country,' said Stelios.

The midday end of school bell rang shrill and loud around the school building. Desks banged shut, papers rattled and the pupils put their blazers on.

'You'll hear all kinds of rumours,' said Carlos. 'What you need to concentrate on is that essay. No excuses, I want your best effort.' The teenagers sat on the edge of their seats looking towards him, waiting. 'Class dismissed.'

In a noisy stream the pupils poured out of the classroom. Carlos put his books in his desk, and his pen and papers in his briefcase. Glancing up, he saw Stelios standing there looking intently at him.

'Excuse me.'

'Yes, Stelios.'

'You're not like the other teachers. We can't trust them and we don't like them,' said Stelios, wide-eyed.

'H'm.'

'You tell us interesting things other teachers don't tell us and you talk in a different way.'

'Well thank you Stelios. I want you to be enthusiastic about your subject, then you'll learn better won't you.'

'Yes, sir.' Stelios hesitated for a few moments, frowned and said, 'Do you think we'll all have to become Muslims?'

Carlos took a deep breath, although the question wasn't a complete surprise. 'Why on earth do you think that?'

'That's what people are saying.'

'I think you can become whatever you want. Keep questioning everything and make up your own mind. That's the answer.'

Stelios stood there, gawping at him admiringly.

'Off you go then, see you Monday with that essay.'

They walked down the corridor.

*

As Carlos came down the steps from the front of the school Raphael crossed the yard and came to him. 'How were your kids today?' said Raphael.

'Good. They're a well-meaning lot, not too much trouble. What about yours?'

Raphael shrugged. 'Easy really except for Abdul; I'm still struggling to keep him in line. Anyway, we're done for the day.'

Noisy children passed by slinging their ragged satchels over their shoulders.

'You still up for the visit?'

'How far is Paradiso?' said Carlos.

'It's in Carabanchel, about forty minutes' walk.'

'Yes, I'm intrigued by what they're up to in there. I think we should see. Let's go.'

In ten minutes they were among the roads and pavements of central Madrid.

'Where are the people? It's like a ghost town, it gives me the creeps,' said Carlos.

'There's nothing here for anyone now,' said Raphael. 'That's why I never come here anymore.'

They passed Gothic grandiose public buildings with some of the windows missing or boarded up. The great edifice of the museum was splattered with graffiti. The streets had a bedraggled, neglected look. They passed a bent man with a shopping trolley full of scrap metal. It clattered and banged noisily as he pushed it over the uneven pavement. Litter was piled up in gutters and there was a smell of rotting fish. Rats scuttled amongst the debris. Where there would have been thin strips of cultivated lawn there was now a wild patchwork of brittle overgrown grass. Further on and into the suburbs was a market place with a few stalls and even fewer people. Bread, jars of jam, some sad looking apples, oranges, grapes and tomatoes were laid out. A few flies buzzed dozily round the produce. The stallholders looked gloomy and dejected. The only people browsing seemed to be workers from nearby offices. Carlos bought an apple.

'Thanks,' said the stallholder. 'You're my first customer today. I don't know how much longer I can carry on. I've got very little stock but even fewer customers.'

Carlos frowned. 'Why can't you get stock?'

'The New Islamic authorities, they've taken over the distribution centres. It's the same for the office workers. They want us all to work for them. I'll have to soon; I've got a family to feed.'

'There's no other way for you to be independent?' Carlos asked.

'No way I know of. It's over for me.'

'I'm sorry,' said Carlos.

They walked on. The few people walking the streets were a cosmopolitan mixture of all colours, races and ages. Some were wearing shabby old clothes; others were better dressed but looked odd in antiquated fashions. The small white terraced houses with shuttered windows looked cheerless and dirty. They walked through suburbs with clear pockets of affluence, smart streets where people had neat front doors and where the smell was fresh. On the windowsills were pots of healthy geraniums. Here men stood on street corners, watching; they looked menacing in their leather jackets. A few blocks further on they passed derelict buildings where bedraggled people sat together silently on doorsteps with expressionless faces like masks, and vacant eyes. A woman in rags with a whining child clinging on to her back thrust a plastic cup at them 'for food, for food.' Just as quickly she wandered off, as if in a daze. They could hear people shouting and there was a smell of garbage. In the roads the gutters trickled with water that was a dirty yellow colour.

'We must be nearing Parque de San Isidro,' said Raphael, 'a tent city.' Around the corner a man lay crumpled in the doorway of an old building, his face red and shimmering in sweat, his shirt and trousers creased and dirty. A young woman knelt beside him.

'Can we help?' said Carlos.

'No, sadly,' said the woman with misery and resignation.

'What's wrong with him?'

'I think he has a chest infection and a broken ankle. I was just passing by. I am a nurse.'

'Then let's get him to the hospital,' said Carlos.

'There's no point. There are too many and not enough medicine.'

'He must be in pain.' Raphael dug into his pocket and pulled out a packet of melt-in-the-mouth paracetamol. 'Give him this. This is the last of my supply.' He knelt down beside the man, stripped out a tablet from the blister and placed it in the man's hand. 'Help him to take it, would you?'

The woman put the tablet gently in the man's mouth.

'Suck this,' she said.

'Then we'll send for a doctor,' said Carlos.

'A doctor will not come out to him.'

'Why not?'

'We have two doctors on duty treating over one hundred people. They can only do so much. Turning to the man she asked, 'Has the tablet dissolved?'

He nodded.

'Then you're going to leave him here?' said Carlos.

'There is nothing else I can do. If you want to take him back to his tent, or wherever he comes from you do it. I deal with this every day. People are left to suffer and die. It is a desperate, desperate situation.' Tears sprang into the nurse's eyes. 'Goodbye.' She quickly walked away.

Carlos watched helplessly as the man wheezed and wheezed and struggled for breath, retched and then was quiet. A long sliver of saliva dripped from the corner of his mouth. For a moment he thought the man was gone, but all of a sudden his leg jerked and he looked at them, bleary eyed.

'We'll take you home, 'said Carlos, 'where do you live?'

'Over there,' he said breathlessly, and pointed towards the tent city. 'Thank you.'

They lifted him, slung one of his arms over each of their shoulders and carried him towards the greyness of tent city. A sheet of blue tarpaulin was fixed to the chain link fence beside the gate. Pinned to it was a notice board, displaying the list of rules.

1.   *No violence.*
2.   *No stealing.*
3.   *Everyone contributes to the upkeep and wellbeing of Parque de San Isidro.*
4.   *No disruptive behaviour.*
5.   *Any disputes to be settled by the authority.*
6.   *No drugs or alcohol.*

Inside was a heaving mass of humanity. There was a great medley of noises; banging, shouting and crying.

'Which way?' asked Raphael.

'Straight ahead.'

Crudely placed flagstones covered the path that led straight into the bowels of Parque de San Isidro. The three of them took up most of the walkway; grubby people had to move out of the way to let them pass. Set off at right angles every twenty-five metres were narrow, litter-strewn alleyways with closely packed tents lined up on either side. On each corner of the row there was an arrow and a sign with a number, like navigation blocks in the centre of a city.

24

Grimy Portaloos were set at the end of each row. Carlos heard one being flushed. Flies swarmed around huge green waste bins with black wheels.

'Which is your row?' asked Carlos.

'Seventeen.'

'So many girls in black,' said Carlos.

'Yes, strange, they can't all be Muslims,' said Raphael.

'I'm sure they're not.'

They moved on. Barefoot bedraggled children played in dirty gutters. Interspersed between tents were improvised structures. A rudimentary hardboard door was attached to a structure made of curtains and tarpaulin propped up by sticks. Written on the door in chalk were the words 'please knock before entering.' Some people had personalised their tents by tying colourful sheets to the posts, like markers. A woman with a broom stopped sweeping as they passed; dust particles wafted high into the warm air. Moving on there was a hot steamy smell; at the side of the path a group of girls were cooking rice in a steel saucepan on an open fire. Through the open doorways they saw grey blankets spread out inside the tents.

'Where is your tent?' asked Carlos.

'Over there, straight on,' the man rasped and jerked his head in the direction.

Nearby was a large arrow suspended on sticks and a sign: 'New Islamic Authority soup kitchen, vouchers needed.' They passed a navigation sign on which 'seventeen' was written. There was a stand pipe in the middle of a path between two rows of tents. People waited in a long queue, mostly old women with a few younger ones, clutching an assortment of pots and pans, some holding plastic containers. There were even a very few boys of nine or ten, all waiting quietly. One small girl came away carrying a large pot half-filled with water. She tripped and fell; the pot rolled some distance away, spilling all of its precious load. The girl got to her feet and collected the empty pot. Her shoulders slumped, and Carlos' heart ached for her as she dejectedly went to the end of the queue, her face full of despair. Carlos and Raphael halted, their burden still slung between them.

'Where to now?' asked Carlos.

The man stood up a little, swaying slightly, but taking more of his weight on his own feet. He tried to speak, but his rasping voice was too faint to be heard. With gestures he directed them down a row of tents, and then to one tent in particular that had a green sheet tied to a pole at the entrance. They stopped.

'Hello,' called Raphael. 'Is anyone there?'

He rapped on the pole with his knuckles. Carlos looked at Raphael; they both shrugged. Raphael pulled aside the fabric that hung like a curtain in front of the entrance, and they took the man inside. They half-carried, half-dragged him to a thin mattress that was lying in one corner and carefully laid him down. Carlos draped a couple of the ubiquitous grey blankets over him. Raphael found a bottle of water and poured some into a battered mug. He held it to the man's lips. The man gulped several mouthfuls and a thin dribble ran down his chin on to the blanket.

'Thank you. And thanks for bringing me home.' His voice was much stronger. 'I'll be all right now.'

'Glad we were able to help,' said Carlos, as he and Raphael left.

On their way out they passed by a woman in black with oriental features who smiled at them.

'Hello. Can you tell me how to get food vouchers?' asked Carlos.

'You must be new here, from Almeira?' she asked in a soft Chinese accent.

'Yes.'

'You need to register with the New Islamic authorities at the mosque. Then they give you a tent, blankets and air mattresses. If you're lucky you'll get one without a hole. Then you work and in exchange you get food vouchers. It's the only way to survive if you're a refugee. You don't have to be a Muslim. They are so nice; they'll talk to you all about Islam. Now I'm convinced that being a Muslim is the only way to be saved.'

'You're not a Muslim, are you?' Carlos said.

'Not by birth, but I am now,' said the woman, her eyes syrupy.

'I see, thanks.' When they reached the entrance Carlos said, 'Shall we do Paradiso? I'm worn out already.' He had a strange feeling of foreboding.

'Yes,' said Raphael, 'I think we should.'

*

Green shoots pushed through the tarmac of the derelict car park outside Paradiso. A few rusty cars were parked in the bays. In the distance was a long queue of people weaving around the huge three-storey building. They were a lively group laughing and joking and their clothes were clean and fresh.

'These people look as if they're from a different planet,' said Carlos.

'Or in a time warp,' added Raphael.

They made their way to the back of the queue.

'It's taken me eight hours to get here, but I don't mind. I'd have travelled for three days if I'd had to,' said one of a pair of women in front of them, breezily. Raphael noticed a sickly sweet scent.

'It's the nail bar I want,' said the other in a singsong voice; she had false eyelashes and bright red lips.

When they got to the front of the queue two burly bouncers stood there, dressed in black.

'Where are your club membership cards?' asked one sharply.

'We're not members but want to join today,' said Carlos.

The bouncer looked at him suspiciously. 'You need to be introduced; this shopping centre is for members only.' He huffed as he looked down at their old shirts and worn out trousers. 'Wait here.' He robustly elbowed them out of the queue and spoke to someone on a walkie-talkie. Carlos and Raphael looked at each other; they were both in unspoken agreement. The moment the bouncer looked the other way they darted around the side of the building.

A man in smart trousers and an expensive looking jacket walked briskly towards them, his eyes feverish.

'I saw you at the front of the queue, being thrown out. If you still want to go in I can help you.'

'Yes, we do' said Carlos.

'Here, have my card,' he said, and thrust it into Carlos' hand. 'You'll both get in on it; I'm never going there again.'

'Why is that?' asked Carlos.

'You'll see when you get inside; I'm going to join the Muslims.'

'Wait,' called Carlos, but just as quickly as he'd appeared, the man was gone.

'What the hell is going on?' asked Raphael.

They queued up again and by the time they got to the front there were different bouncers on duty and with the card the new ones let them in. At the cloakroom people were giving in their jackets, shawls and bags and collecting a token. Underneath their plain outer garments women were dressed in exotic, colourful, skimpy clothes, men in expensive shirts. There was a palpable sense of excitement. As they entered the cool air hit them like a slap.

'My God, air con,' said Raphael.

There was taped music. A jingly, catchy little tune repeated: 'If you want it, you can have it,' over and over again. There was a large billboard above hanging on chains: 'Happiness is retail therapy - indulge yourself, you deserve it,' in large colourful Broadway script.

'What is this place? It looks like a theme park,' said Carlos.

The three floors were connected with escalators going up and down and a large atrium. It looked bright and clean. People were thronging everywhere and there were shops bursting with merchandise.

'I haven't seen so much stuff for years,' said Carlos. 'How the hell have they kept this place secret?'

The women from the queue disappeared into a shop called 'Me, Me, Me. Nail bar!' Next to that was a shop called 'On Trend Glamour', advertising real hair extensions and wigs. Inside it excited women fondled the samples. Next door to that was a leather shop. In the window were snakeskin bags and shoes from East Africa and a slogan 'Buy it Before it's Extinct!' On the other side of the walkway, swarming with people, men were crowded round an auctioneer. He was auctioning off smartphones, gadgets on tripods and cameras. They were fetching exorbitant prices.

'I didn't think you could get hold of that stuff,' said Raphael.

'Seems like they want them at any price,' said Carlos. 'There's no shortage of money in here.'

'A fool and his money are soon parted,' said Raphael.

Raphael began to feel sick. He saw Carlos' jaw dropping open. People were loitering in the walkways, some were getting excited and some scuffles broke out. There was an atmosphere of urgency, like a mad sale, except there were no bargains that they could see. They passed a bridal shop where a girl was looking at a dress.

'But Carla had six petticoats under her dress and this one only has four.' She stomped her foot like a belligerent child.

'But it's still very pretty,' said the mother.

A man with a megaphone walked towards them, a billboard strung over his chest; on it was a photograph of a woman wearing almost nothing except a seductive smile. He announced: 'Visit our superb new state of the art complex on the lower concourse. Treat yourself to a swim and a post swim pampering. No water shortage in here.' They took the escalator to the lower concourse. The reception area sparkled with neon lights and there were rails of glittery swimwear and goggles for sale. Raphael could see Carlos was agitated. He watched as Carlos walked straight up to one of the receptionists. She had peroxide hair piled high in a beehive, a fake tan and heavy makeup. Her many bracelets jingled.

'Do you know, people outside don't have enough water for the bare necessities of life? They're not people in remotest, darkest Africa, they're Spaniards like you, and they're right here,' he said with a passionate intensity.

The receptionist's plastic smile morphed into a vindictive sneer.

'Piss off do-gooder,' she said savagely. 'I can see by the way you dress you're not one of us. Go and join the riff-raff outside. They, like you, belong in the gutter.'

Carlos looked at her in stunned silence.

'Come on, cool it. We're only here to gather information,' said Raphael, dragging Carlos away by the arm.

They travelled on the escalator up to the middle concourse. There was a savoury smell. They passed a billboard advertising today's speciality, 'Crispy wild duck from Taiwan in lemon and dill sauce.' The restaurant was called 'The Discerning Gourmet'. They looked through the window. Obsequious waiters in crisp white suits walked up and down expertly balancing plates of steaming hot food. The savoury smell was stronger here. Carlos hovered around the open entrance while a waiter with an ingratiating smile looked them up and down. Raphael could see he was not impressed by their attire but decided it wasn't as important as the colour of their money. After considering for a few moments he invited them in.

'Where do you get your duck from?' asked Carlos.

'Why Taiwan of course, sir.'

'How can you? There's no transport to and from Taiwan,' said Carlos frowning.

The waiter gave a facetious smirk. 'If you know the right people there will always be transport.'

'Out there, there's no transport for necessities for those poor bastards,' said Carlos.

'Money and connections are the currency in here,' he replied; a speck of spit flew out of his mouth and landed on Carlos' shirt. The waiter sneered at them, turned away and tried to entice some other customers into the restaurant.

'Come on,' said Raphael.

They passed a man's clothes shop, 'Haute Couture Chic.' They stared at the manikin in the window, dressed in a coat. 'Figure hugging sensual onyx black coat with mulberry trim. The ultimate stylish look.' Inside the shop Raphael saw a frantic-looking man; he was trying to negotiate with the shop assistant a reduction for a designer shirt. An argument broke out and the manager was called. He looked at the customer in disgust, grabbed him roughly by the arm, pulled him out of the shop and pushed him to the ground.

'Look, if you're in here and you've got no money you're a bloody nobody. You may as well be dead,' said the manager.

The man fell to his knees in the walkway. Raphael watched Carlos follow the manager into the shop and shout furiously, 'You already are dead!'

31

Raphael looked down at the crumpled man with a mixture of pity, bafflement and contempt.

'You don't really need that shirt, do you?' asked Raphael.

'I must have that shirt,' he said, like a desperate child.

When Carlos came out of the shop Raphael saw his face was like thunder. They wandered on. The next space was a casino with roulette tables and female croupiers dressed in skimpy bikinis dealing blackjack. Beyond that was an enormous billboard promoting 'The Pleasure Dome.' There were shrieks of laughter. Swarms of inebriated men and women staggered in and out. They passed by a man with a megaphone announcing in a melodious voice: 'Visit our image specialist. Half price offer today at Feline beauty shop on the middle concourse. Impress your friends and explore your dreams.' In the walkway two women were having an argument over a cocktail dress they'd snatched from a rail of clothes. They were both pulling on it like a rope in a tug of war. 'It's mine, I saw it first,' said one woman baring her teeth. 'Get your hands off it,' said the other. Perched on top of the rail and suspended with a vertical pin was a sign; 'Buy me now or lose me forever.' Raphael was absorbed in watching the fight with a sort of sickly fascination when he felt Carlos dig him in the ribs with his elbow.

'Look, am I really seeing this?' Carlos said.

In front of them was an A-frame walkway board advertising: 'Legs, bums and tums, cosmetic surgery for you today.' They read the smaller print. 'Yes, you can still have it all. Get your face lift, nose job, breast enhancement, tummy tuck, liposuction here – no questions asked. Qualified doctors will give you their individual attention.' Raphael felt his jaw drop open. A man walked breezily out of the doorway with a plaster on his nose. A woman being wheeled out in a chair had an enormous bandage around her midriff.

'Right,' said Carlos, 'keep quiet and I'll do the talking.'

They walked straight into the reception area decorated with a thick pink carpet and an ornate chandelier. A fountain of water made a soothing sound as it trickled over a rock feature. There was a smell of sweet perfume. The walls were lined with row upon row of before and after photographs of satisfied customers, with close ups of noses, breasts, stomachs and legs. There were a few customers looking at the photographs. A man whose nose was too perfect and whose teeth were too white encouraged them to sit down in the soft leather chairs and discuss their needs. As they sat down the chairs gave off a luxurious hiss. Written on his name badge was 'Dr Antonio Andreas'. He introduced himself.

'I've never been happy with my nose,' said Carlos. 'I'd like a nose job.'

'Of course,' said Dr Andreas sycophantically. 'It's a very simple procedure and after the other doctors have done a few simple medical checks we can do it for you today. We have plenty of medication and offer first rate aftercare. In fact if your friend is interested we have a special offer this week only; have one nose done and a friend gets one half price.'

Carlos leapt out of the chair, grabbed the doctor by the tie, pulled him so close that their noses were almost touching and eyeballed him. Raphael saw the doctor's terrified expression.

'There are people dying from lack of medical attention out there and you're wasting your time in here on useless procedures for selfish, vain people,' Carlos said. 'You're a disgrace to your profession.'

'I... I... ' gasped the doctor with terror in his eyes.

Carlos pushed him roughly back and he fell into the chair where he lay awkwardly with his legs splayed, spluttering and choking.

'They're brainwashed out there and they're mesmerised in here: isn't anybody awake?' exclaimed Carlos, furiously.

Raphael was worried. He'd never seen Carlos so wild before. Carlos ran out into the walkway with Raphael in hot pursuit. Carlos grabbed the megaphone from the man advertising the image change and like a lightning bolt zipped up the escalator travelling towards the upper concourse.

'Wake up, wake up you shoppers! You're in a conditioned sleep. You're just doing what the advertising tells you to do,' he shouted into the megaphone, his voice at fever pitch.

'Stop him!' yelled a man in a designer suit who jumped onto the escalator after him.

'Your hair extensions, fancy food, designer coats and false breasts are just a veneer. Your greed for material things is a bottomless pit. They'll never bring lasting satisfaction or happiness.' Three burly bouncers dressed in black rushed after him, ruthlessly pushing their way through the crowds. When he reached the top he whizzed across the walkway and down the escalator on the other side. He shouted furiously into the megaphone. 'They're illusions! Your lives are vacuous! Beneath your pretentious veneer you're insecure and narcissistic. You're incapable of loving yourself or others.' With an enormous leap he hurdled over the side of the escalator and landed on the walkway of the second concourse.

Someone shouted, 'Get the madman out!'

Four or five bouncers chased frantically after him. Shoppers looked bemused by the incident unfolding before them. 'That's why you're ignoring the grinding poverty of the people outside. Inside each one of you is an authentic person trying to get out, but carry on the way you are and you'll wither and die.' Raphael saw people gawp at Carlos uncomprehendingly, as if he were speaking in a foreign language. 'We're all in this together. The planet doesn't care about humanity; we're just a blip on the surface of time.'

The bouncers had reached Carlos and one grabbed the megaphone. Carlos was a long way away now and Raphael was just able to see him surrounded by the group of men in black. Carlos' arms were pulled back and handcuffs were snapped onto his wrists before he was led away. The people quickly went back to their shopping. Raphael's heart thumped and he trembled a little. Oh God, oh God, I must find out where he's gone, he said to himself. He walked aimlessly round the concourse thinking, thinking. He recognised one of the bouncers who had taken Carlos away. The man leaned on the aluminium rail and looked lazily down into the atrium. Raphael stood next to him and looked downwards.

'Pity that madman managed to get in,' Raphael said.

'Yeah, people want to shop, they don't want disturbances,' he said nonchalantly.

'They've taken him away I hope.'

'Yes, they've handed him over to the New Islamic authorities; he'll be locked up with the others.'

'Good,' said Raphael, 'but why the New Islamic authorities, he's of no interest to them, is he?'

'He's a trouble-maker.'

'I'm curious why the New Islamic authorities allow this shopping centre, you know, when they're so strict with their rules?'

The bouncer looked wryly at him. 'Keep this to yourself but Imam Ali comes here after hours. He likes the food, the pool and a bit of roulette as well. He's got loads of the stuff.' He rubbed his thumb and his fingers together. 'Can't get him off the table, I hear.'

Raphael's eyes widened. 'A bit hypocritical isn't it, one set of rules for those living hand to mouth in the streets and another for those in here with money?'

'Well, what do I care? I'm earning a living of sorts and I'm in the air-conditioning all day. You've got to look after yourself.'

'Sure,' said Raphael, and walked away. He made his way back to the city and stopped briefly at the top of a hill. There was a foul smell of decay in the air. There below him lay the grey amorphous wasteland of tent city which seemed to tremble with agitated life; a seething mass of dispossessed humanity. He felt his body quiver and his hands became tight fists. He could feel his nails sinking painfully into the palms of his hands.

With a wordless cry of anguish he yelled out to the horizon and kneeling, fell exhausted with his head forward on the dusty ground. Tears welled in his eyes.

CHAPTER 4

An Lac ashram, Switzerland

'May I join you?' Without waiting for an answer Erin plopped her plate down on the wooden table in the bright sun and perched herself at one end of the bench, next to Jane. She smiled across at Ahmed who gave a nod of greeting. Jane grunted something unintelligible and moved along slightly, giving Erin more room.

'I'm absolutely famished,' said Erin, spearing a glistening carrot with her fork. 'Ahmed, may I trouble you for some water please?'

Ahmed filled a cup with water from an earthenware jug and, giving a slight smile, handed the cup to Erin. Looking down into the valley Erin saw Stefano walking toward the barn with a chicken under his arm.

'Thanks.' Erin took a long swallow of the cool water. 'Mm, I love the water from our well. It always tastes so fresh, especially on a hot day like this.' She noticed Jane staring at her with a hard look. 'What?'

'Ahmed's fasting,' hissed Jane, eyes narrowed under the floppy brimmed hat.

'Really?' said Erin. 'It's not Ramadan, is it Ahmed? I thought it's in November this year.'

'You're right, Ramadan is in November. No, I'm just fasting for a day or two. Last year I missed a couple of days of fasting during Ramadan because I was travelling. Now I'm making them up.'

'And here I am, eating and drinking in front of you and you're trying to fast! I'm very sorry.'

An Alpine swift flew on to the patio and pecked around her feet.

'Honestly Erin, it's all right.'

'Well, if you're sure... '

'Yes, of course,' he waved his arm encouragingly in the direction of the food, 'enjoy.'

'Are you not eating, Jane? You're not fasting as well, are you?'

'No, but I thought it would be insensitive to sit here eating while Ahmed's fasting.'

'That's very thoughtful of you, but you don't need to bother on my account, honestly.'

Erin ate a couple of mouthfuls of the almond roast, one of her favourite meals from the dining hall. The texture was deliciously nutty and it tasted of basil, garlic and tomatoes.

'So, Ahmed, presumably you always fast during Ramadan each year?' Erin asked.

'No, actually I don't. Not for all thirty days anyway. Sometimes I'm travelling, like last year, and I don't make up the days. Sometimes - well to be honest, sometimes I just don't bother to do the whole month. Although I do always fast for some of the time.'

'What about Adeena? Does she always fast?'

'My wife is more pious than I. She always does the whole thing. Always has, even as a child, although young children are normally exempted.'

The swift flew up and perched on the edge of the table. Erin threw it a piece of bread from her plate; it pecked it into its beak and flew away.

'I hear it's compulsory in many places now, where the New Islamists are in charge,' said Erin. 'Even if you're not Muslim, you have to take part. It's not just fasting either, is it? You have to do all the other stuff as well - no alcohol, praying five times a day, everything.'

'Yes,' sighed Ahmed. 'That is wrong, to force people against their wishes. It's too extreme. And I believe it's against true Islam. You can't really be a true Muslim if you're coerced into it. And you're not a true Muslim if you coerce others.'

'And they say they're just trying to be true to their faith' said Jane.

'Yes, but it's a distortion.'

'The New Islamists seem to be taking over everywhere,' said Jane.

'Not everywhere yet, thank goodness,' said Ahmed. 'There are still places, even now, where moderate Muslims prevail, and there are some areas where faith is not seen as important. And of course Annando's ideas about living in harmony with each other are spreading more widely all the time. I'm so glad to be at An Lac: from here we can make a real difference.'

'If the New Islamists don't winkle us out of our hiding place and destroy us,' said Jane. 'You weren't with us when we had to leave Austria a few years ago were you, Ahmed?'

'No, I had not joined you then, although I had seen Annando once, in Italy. He gave an outstanding speech, and I am not a man who's easily impressed. What a revelation, he spoke such piercing truths. I'd never met anyone like him. He inspired me, touched me to the core. Adeena was touched too.'

'So many people feel the same the first time they hear him,' said Jane.

'I spoke to a friend of mine afterwards, a studious, pious man and he said to me "I've been wrong, all of my life. I listen to this man and now I see the light." What a thing to say.'

Erin bit hungrily into her bread and swallowed a couple of mouthfuls then spoke. 'That's why the New Islamists fear him so much.'

'He's the one holding it all together - he's really our only hope,' said Jane thoughtfully.

'I'm not so sure about that,' said Erin. 'According to Maurice in our latest meeting Annando's message has been taken up by many people - groups are starting up everywhere. It may be taking on a life of its own. I hope so, because he can't keep going for ever. One day he won't be with us... although let's hope that day is a long way off.'

'Yes, let us hope,' said Jane, fervently. 'Luckily Sunnido does a brilliant job of looking after him, making sure he takes his medication on time, nagging him to take enough exercise and the rest of it.'

'Sunnido's been his assistant for a long time, I believe. Is that right?' asked Ahmed.

'Since before most of us in An Lac were born,' said Erin. 'They met in Vietnam in the 1960s, during the war. At one time they were both monks at a Buddhist monastery there. That's why you always see the two of them wearing saffron robes. The monastery in Vietnam was also called An Lac.'

'The first time I saw Annando I knew I was going to see a Buddhist monk but I was surprised to find that he is an Englishman. What's his background?'

'Nobody knows very much about his past, really. He doesn't talk about it. We have just snippets of information, from things that have been mentioned over the years,' said Erin. 'Apparently he was seriously injured while visiting An Lac: the Viet Cong were all over the place in those days. Sunnido nursed him back to health and after about three years he returned to London. He got some sort of high-powered job for a few years then chucked it in, went back to An Lac and became a Buddhist monk.'

'Amazing. Do you know what sort of job he had?'

'He was a scientist, doing applied research in physics.'

'How extraordinary. What else do you know?'

'When Annando returned the old abbot, Ajahn Kai Luat, trained Annando to take over from him. He died a short time later. Annando was the youngest abbot they'd ever had.'

'He must have been very exceptional.'

'He still is. None of us have met anyone remotely like him.'

'Who will take over after Annando, here or wherever we find ourselves?'

'That's a good question Ahmed, but no one knows the answer: Annando hasn't chosen a successor.'

'This is morbid,' said Jane frowning. She tilted the hat to shield her face from the sun. 'Talking of Annnado as though he's already passed away. Do you have to discuss it now?'

'I think we have to be practical. It's important to know the direction in which we're headed. We need a leader to keep the momentum going as these groups develop and build their communities.'

'Adeena and I are here because Annando is so inspiring. We believe strongly in Annando's teaching that it is vital for everyone to progress in spiritual development irrespective of their faith tradition or lack of it. I would like to learn more about these communities, your utopia.'

'It's not a utopia like previous ones such as Robespierre or Hitler or Stalin, which of course all failed,' said Erin.

'Why did they fail?'

'Because they were based on flawed ideologies.'

'What ideologies?' Ahmed leant towards Erin, his serious face full of concentration.

'Robespierre wanted a moral and incorruptible society, Hitler wanted a racially pure one. Stalin wanted a disciplined and classless one. An Lac's vision is of networks of small communities. We start by valuing each and every individual. Our communities will be based on equality, tolerance and a sense of belonging where people do things for each other rather than for material gain.'

'It sounds good, but how will the communities work?' Ahmed asked.

'These will be as self-sufficient as possible and use resources as sustainably as they can. Each community will cooperate with ones nearby, pooling assets and resources as needed.'

'But when the communities expand won't they just turn into towns and cities like before?'

'No. Once a community reaches a certain size a new small community will be founded. We regard the incessant drive to create larger and larger cities to have been a huge mistake. The future lies in well-ordered small communities where everyone is following a spiritual path. Only that way can we even hope to live in harmony.'

'That's a bold idea but I like the sound of it. The more I learn about Annando and An Lac the more certain I am that Adeena and I have found our spiritual home.' Ahmed frowned and looked down at Erin's plate. 'But I'm sorry, keeping you talking and letting your food get cold.'

'I don't mind,' said Erin. 'It's just as good cold or hot.' She quickly finished off the last few mouthfuls and put her knife and fork neatly in the centre of her plate. 'Tilly!' Erin called. A young girl of about ten years' old, her blonde hair in dangling plaits, approached the table.

'Yes, Erin?'

'Tilly, please would you do me a big favour and take my plate and glass back to the kitchen for me, I have to run some errands.'

Tilly nodded and scampered off, carrying the plate and glass firmly with both hands.

'Who's that?' asked Ahmed. 'There are so many children here I find it difficult to keep track of who is who.'

'That's one of my daughters,' said Jane.

Erin stood up. 'Ahmed, it's good to have you and Adeena with us at An Lac. Now if you will excuse me there are some matters I must attend to.'

Erin strode briskly away.

CHAPTER 5

The front door burst open with a bang. Ralph felt a stream of cool fresh air; he peered over the rim of his half-moon reading glasses. Tom stood in the doorway.

'Mum, Dad, listen, Erin is going to Madrid to rescue Carlos and I'm going with her.' His eyes darted from Ralph to Jane and back to Ralph.

Jane stared at Tom, frowned and quietly resumed scrubbing, thrusting her yellow rubber-gloved hands deep in the frothy sink; the water sloshed and the crockery clinked. Ralph sat forward in his armchair and closed his newspaper. Slowly he folded it in half, then in half again and placed it on top of the pile of clean laundry lying on the floor beside him.

'Out of the way and let me in,' Erin pushed past Tom and closed the front door behind her with a soft click; Tom moved aside.

'Erin.' Ralph put his reading glasses on the newspaper. 'What exactly is going on?'

'Annando agrees it's a good idea for me to go to Madrid, and if possible get Carlos out. I need someone with me and we discussed various people; Annando suggested Tom. I don't mind telling you I was very surprised at that idea, but I have given it a lot of thought and I am prepared to take him. He's strong and resilient, and he can speak a little Spanish. There have to be certain conditions, though.'

'What are they?' said Ralph.

'Tom has to be straight with me and reliable. I've got to be able to trust him and he has to carry out my instructions exactly and willingly at all times.'

Tom burst out, 'You can trust me, Erin. I'll do exactly as you say. I promise.'

'So, it's all arranged then is it?' Ralph said, 'without consulting his parents?'

'That's why we're here now. I thought about it and checked that Tom wanted to go.'

'Of course he would,' snorted Ralph. 'I'm not sure, just the two of you... '

'Hank will be driving us up to the border with France. He'll make sure we get off to a good start. You know he's very reliable. Obviously you two have the final say: if you say no, Tom stays here. I'm leaving tomorrow if I can, let me know.'

Erin went out and shut the door behind her.

'Well, Dad? Mum?'

'Let me think,' said Ralph. Keeping Tom away from Isabella would certainly be a good thing, and was probably one of the factors that Erin had considered when making her decision. But could Tom be relied upon not to do something stupid and jeopardise the whole mission? Was he prepared to allow Tom to be sent into danger like this? 'I'm not sure.'

'Erin is,' said Tom quickly.

'She doesn't know you as well as your mother and I do. You don't have a good track record of reliability and I'm not sure you're mature enough.'

'I'm seventeen. That's mature.'

'How often have you acted as though you're mature? It's not a question of age; it's a question of reliability, dependability, etc. These last few months you've caused your mother and me a lot of worry with all the things you've done. You've been defiant, argumentative and impetuous, so it's no surprise that I'm not brimming with confidence about you going.'

As Jane drained the sink the water gushed down the hole with a loud swirling suck.

'Maybe we should give him a chance, Ralph.' She picked up a tea towel and dried a plate from the pile.

'Come on, Dad. My life here is so dull, cooped up in the ashram, seeing the same people day in day out for month after month. I need a change. This will be a challenge.'

'He's right; he's like a caged bird. Give him a chance to fly free,' said Jane.

'This isn't a game, nor a character-building exercise. This mission is deadly serious.' Ralph had a hot itchy feeling; he shifted his position in the chair. 'You don't get a second chance. You have to get everything right first time.'

Tom clenched his fists. 'I know that and I want to go.'

'You're likely to do something irresponsible and ruin the whole thing. Probably with some girl or other.'

'Please, Dad. I'll show you how responsible I can be.'

'Respect has got to be earned.'

'I know, and I will earn it, I promise you.'

Ralph frowned, sat back in his chair and scrutinised Tom. 'I've heard your promises before.'

'Dad, you say I've been irresponsible, and maybe I have. This is my chance to prove to you that I can change. Please let me go.' He looked over at Jane. 'Tell him, Mum.'

'Ralph, I think we should let him go,' said Jane quietly.

Tom's piercing and defiant look became more and more intense. He thrust his shoulders back.

'Look, this mission needs me. I don't care what you think. Even if you say no, I'm going anyway.'

Ralph winced and burst into a sharp, abrupt laugh.

'You see?' he shouted. 'This is exactly why I think you'd be a liability. Erin needs a reliable adult, not an impetuous child.' Ralph jumped to his feet. 'You just can't turn it off, can you?'

'Be reasonable, the pair of you. Why is it always like this?' Jane clapped the tea towel over the sink, where it lay like an abused rag doll; and dashed out of the room.

Tom waved his fists in the air, his eyes blazing. 'OK, OK, I was wrong to say that. Just let me go Dad, please.'

It crossed Ralph's mind that if he said no, living with Tom would be even more of a trial than before. Tom would be devastated, crushed and permanently angry: hell to live with. On the other hand this journey could be the making of him. And Ralph had been impressed with his sincere determination to prove himself. He heaved a deep sigh, and nodded. 'All right,' he said.

'Wow, thanks Dad. You won't regret it.' Tom sped out of the room faster than a speeding jackal, and shot up the stairs.

'I'm already regretting it,' whispered Ralph.

CHAPTER 6

Erin, Tom and Hank scrambled down a steep slope to the trail snaking through the trees. Droplets of rainwater hung precariously on the ends of pine needles and the earth glistened wetly. Erin breathed in the sharp fresh scent, she felt it travel down her nostrils into her throat and could taste its tangy flavour. Rounding a bend in the trail Hank stopped in front of a small wood panelled hut. It looked no different from all the other huts dotted throughout the mountains used for shelter by forest rangers. This must be it, thought Erin. Hank unlocked the padlock on the front door. As he pulled it back the hinges squeaked; he went inside, closing the door behind him. There was a loud click, the whole front of the hut swung open; a red Fiat car nestled inside. Quickly Hank drove the car out of its hiding place, Erin and Tom got in, Hank closed the hut, got behind the wheel and they sped off.

'It's a reliable piece of junk,' said Hank.

'It is with your attention and technical knowhow; it must be a lot older than Tom.'

Hank patted the dashboard and smiled. After driving down the track for four kilometres they reached a tarmac road. Hank stopped the car, leaned forwards and looked carefully in all directions.

'Seems deserted to me,' said Erin. 'Nobody around to see where we've come from.'

'I think you're right,' said Hank, easing the Fiat forward on to the road. With no further need for secrecy he switched from electric motor to diesel engine. A faint acrid odour from the recycled cooking oil fuel seeped into the car.

Sandwiched on the back seat between two heavily-laden rucksacks Tom had a huge grin on his face. Erin frowned at him.

'What are you grinning about?'

'We're out – no longer cooped up in An Lac, in danger of being discovered by New Islamists. It's so good to be free at last.'

'This isn't a joyride, you know. We have got to trek across Switzerland, France and half of Spain and get to Madrid without getting robbed or killed. Then we're supposed to liberate Carlos from wherever it is they're holding him, without getting shot or arrested ourselves. Then we've got to get him back to An Lac. We'll have help from contacts in the network along the way, but none of it's going to be easy. In fact it's bloody difficult and dangerous as hell. You're sitting there grinning like a Cheshire cat as though it's all just a jolly adventure.'

'Erin, I know it might be dangerous but we're still in Switzerland. This is the safest bit. We're in the mountains. The sun is shining, the sky is blue, the scenery is beautiful. Can't we enjoy at least some of the journey?'

'He's got a point, you know,' said Hank.

'Yes, I know he has. I'm just a bit on edge, that's all.'

'We do need to lighten up, otherwise you'll be a nervous wreck before we get there,' said Tom.

They drove on, not talking. There was little other traffic: a number of battered lorries with blue tarpaulin-covered loads, some private cars with one or two occupants. Shortly before midday they had to wait a few minutes in a short queue of traffic. The noise of a thundering drill pierced the air.

'What the hell is that racket?' said Tom, his teeth on edge.

Later they passed some bulky machinery and men wearing high-visibility jackets repairing the road.

A few kilometres further they stopped at a deserted clearing where a few wooden tables with benches were set out. Erin put the picnic Jane had prepared on the table.

'I'm going to miss Daisy the cow's produce,' said Tom as he took out the stiff strips of cheese smeared in red chutney from the sandwiches and munched them down followed by the heavy dark wholemeal bread. There were a few carrot chunks and a thermos of coffee. Tom reached into the bag for more food.

'No, Tom,' said Erin. 'We need to conserve our supplies.'

'It'll be less to carry.'

'Nice try Tom, but no. We don't know for sure how long this food will have to last us.'

With a sigh Tom put the bag down.

In the late afternoon Hank pulled in to a stopping place by the side of the road.

'This is it,' he said. 'If you go up that rise there's a dirt track that leads further up the mountain. The border with France is about two kilometres along the track. You shouldn't have any trouble getting across. Good luck.'

Erin embraced him; he smelt of tomato chutney and coffee.

'Thanks for everything, Hank.'

Hank smiled and stuck out his hand to Tom. Tom felt Hank's calloused hand warm and strong.

'Take care, young man.' He turned to Erin. 'I'll buy a round of drinks when the two of you get back with Carlos.'

'I'll hold you to it.'

Tom and Erin swung their rucksacks on to their backs and set off.

'What's he mean?' asked Tom. 'No-one uses money at An Lac - everything's free.'

'Just an old expression. I'll explain it to you sometime. For now though let's save our breath for walking.'

Erin felt the cool mountain air on her cheeks. Looking around 360 degrees were mountains with snow peaks and long lush grass. In the distance cow bells tinkled. The deserted border was marked with a small metal sign attached to a wooden post 'Bienvenue en France', the sentry post abandoned. Peering through the window Tom saw litter and empty bottles of beer strewn over the floor, faded official notices were pinned to the wall. After walking a few more kilometres they found a sheltered spot, a short distance from the path. The ground was covered in short downy grass surrounded by Scots pine trees, rhododendron ferrugineum and a few colourful dwarf orchids. About thirty metres away the ground sloped down to form the bank of a wide mountain stream. They set up their tents and put their mats and sleeping bags inside. Tom gobbled up the rest of the sandwiches washed down with Jane's cloudy apple juice. Erin suddenly stood up.

'I'm going to have a wash in the stream. You stay here and keep an eye on things.'

She scrambled down the bank and was soon out of sight. Tom waited a few minutes and then crept quietly to the edge of the overhang. Taking cover behind a large rock he peered into the dip below. He could see Erin midstream, crouched down and scooping handfuls of water over herself. After a few moments she stood up. Tom gasped as he saw that she was naked. Her rounded hips and stomach were bathed in the warm rosy glow of the rays from the setting sun. She had full breasts and her nipples stood hard and proud. Tom's mouth opened slightly, and his breath came in short gasps. Erin turned her head and looked in his direction.

'Tom', she called, 'go back to the camp. Now!'

How did she know I was there? he wondered as he slunk back to the tents. Dressed, Erin came and stood over where Tom sat in front of his tent.

'When I told you to keep an eye on things that wasn't an invitation to spy on me having a bath. Now you go and have a cold bath yourself. If that isn't enough to cool you down, you'd better have a wank before you come back to camp. Now off you go.'

Tom stood naked beside the stream, trying to get up enough courage to plunge into the icy water. He stepped in, the water came to his knees. He could feel his toes going numb already. The shiver that had started in his feet shot through his body until he quaked all over. Quickly he sat down, and gasped with the cold, his heart racing. He scooped up handfuls of water and splashed them over himself like he had seen Erin do. Thoughts of Erin brought back to mind the image of her standing naked in the stream. He got out and stood shivering on the bank, his hard erect penis bobbing. Tom dried himself quickly then dropped his towel on the grass and took hold of his erection. As he stroked himself he recalled the sight of Erin splashing herself, then standing naked and unselfconscious in the sunlight. After a few minutes Tom shuddered as he climaxed. Spunk gushed out of him and fell into the stream, swept away by the fast current. He cleaned himself up, dressed quickly and climbed up the bank. When he got to the camp, Erin was seated by her tent. She looked up.

'Sit down, Tom, I want to say something to you.'

Shamefacedly Tom sat down and waited, avoiding her gaze.

'Now, Tom, I know that you've had a number of girlfriends at An Lac. Like any normal teenager you're eager to have sex as often as you can. You're a young man, and I am a woman. However, I am off-limits. There will be no sexual contact between you and me – none at all. Control yourself. If you have any fantasies about me and put a hand on me... in that way... I will break your fingers. Is that clear?'

Tom nodded, reddening. He knew that Erin wouldn't actually harm him in that way, but he didn't want to find out what she would really do to him.

'Right, that's settled then. Let's get some sleep. We'll make an early start tomorrow. Goodnight.'

'Goodnight, Erin.'

*

Next morning shortly after dawn they had bagels with lashings of apple jam made from the orchard at An Lac, and broke camp. There was no mention of the previous night's incident, although Tom had expected Erin to refer to it. He now saw that this was Erin's way of doing things: identify a problem, take action to sort it out and then move on, without dwelling on the past. Tom knew that Erin had a reputation at An Lac for being an outstandingly capable administrator, and he was beginning to see why.

After a couple of hours descending the mountain they came to a tarmac road. They stopped to rest for a few minutes while Erin studied the map before striding along the road, going south. Soon they came to a road sign saying 'Maranz' and entered a small village, its neat terraced houses arranged around the village square. In the centre of the square was a disused fountain, its granite bowl cracked. A small lorry, battered but sturdy, was parked in the shade of a parched almond tree. Beside the lorry was a man in dark blue overalls securing the blue tarpaulin at the side, wrapping its rope around a metal stanchion, and tying it off. Finished, he opened the door of the driver's cab and climbed inside. Erin darted forward.

'Excusez-moi,' she said in her best French.

'Yes?' he said in English with a French accent. His voice was deep with a ragged heavy quality to it.

Why do they always do that, she wondered, mentally shrugged and switched to English.

'You're not going south, are you?'

52

The man was silent for a few moments, looking at Erin, taking her in. His face brightened.

'You're in luck, I am.'

'Would you mind giving us a lift, please? If you could take us some of the way there, we'd be very thankful.'

'Put your gear in the back and jump in.'

At the back of the lorry Erin held up a corner of the tarpaulin, while Tom stowed the rucksacks inside.

'Tom,' Erin whispered, 'if he asks where we're going and what for, let me do all the talking, OK?'

'OK.'

'This is very good of you, to give us a lift,' Erin said, as she and Tom climbed aboard. Inside there was a strong smell of Gauloise. A small liqueur bottle with string tied round its neck hung from a hook above the windscreen.

'Oh that's all right, I'm going there anyway. I like to have company. That is if you're not escaped lunatics from the local asylum.' He smiled.

'Is there an asylum near here then?' asked Tom, startled.

'No.'

'Oh.' Tom tried to cover his embarrassment by staring out of the side window.

'When we stowed our bags in the back I noticed a smell of fish,' said Erin. 'You don't bring fish from the coast all the way up here, do you?'

The driver laughed.

'I do deliver fish,' he said, 'north of Marseilles. It's too far to bring them in my lorry up here. You need proper refrigerated lorries for that. They're too expensive for me. No, I've been visiting relatives in the village for a few days. My name's Pierre, by the way.'

'I'm Sarah and this is my nephew, Paul.' Tom sat straight in his seat, his ears pricked up. 'We're planning to visit relatives too. My cousin, he lives in Cassis.'

'Ah yes, the new port, now that Marseilles is half under water. Tragedy, that. Complete tragedy. Did you know Marseilles, before the sea rose and half-drowned it?'

'No, I've never been.'

'A pity. It was a lovely city. Hundreds of years of history, gone just like that.' He shook his head.

'Yes, so many places are now submerged. It's very sad. And so quickly too.'

'Yes, everyone was saying sea levels would rise, but gradually, over many years. But after that asteroid smashed into the ice sheet in Antarctica…'

'It didn't,' said Tom.

'Didn't what?' said Pierre.

'The asteroid - it didn't hit the ground at all. We studied it in school. It exploded in mid-air. Went off with the power of scores of atomic bombs. That's what broke up the Pine Island ice sheet, creating half a dozen country-sized icebergs. It was the melting of those that made the sea rise so quickly, in less than ten years.'

'Well, the effect was devastating, whether it hit or not,' said Pierre gruffly.

'Of course we were headed for an ecological disaster anyway,' said Tom.

'Because of man's activities?'

'Yep, our obsession with burning fossil fuels, filling the atmosphere with CO_2 and causing global warming. For millennia Earth was a sleeping giant geologically, but in the last few decades the warming woke it, producing loads more earthquakes and volcanic eruptions. And extreme weather, floods and droughts everywhere. We destroyed whole ecosystems with our system of linear use of resources.'

'What do you mean, linear use of resources?'

'It's the way mankind operates, it's so destructive. Natural processes tend to go in cycles, there's the carbon cycle, the nitrogen cycle, water cycle, lots of them. We've pushed these out of balance. Also we snatch raw materials out of the ground and the seas, consume them and then dump the residue. We treat the earth as a giant rubbish tip.'

'So the planet was doomed anyway?'

'No, not the planet,' said Tom earnestly. 'Earth will go on regardless; it's our civilisation that faces doom.'

They sat quietly for a while. 'What does your cousin do, in Cassis?'

There was a moment's delay before Erin answered. Tom stiffened and his mind raced.

'He used to live in Marseilles but when the sea level rose too high he had to leave, like so many others. Now he's got an oyster fishery just down the coast from Cassis,' said Erin, in a chatty relaxed tone.

Tom took a deep breath, listening intently.

'Oh really? I don't deal in oysters myself, but I know some of the fishermen. What's his name?'

'Daniel Fournier. Do you know him?'

'Not personally, no, but I have heard the name. Good chap, they say. Hard worker. Well, well it's a small world, isn't it?'

'It certainly is.'

'Fewer people now though,' said Tom.

'Since the epidemic you mean?' said Erin.

'Yes.'

'I lost my wife and two sons to the epidemic,' said Pierre quietly. 'Thanks to those bastards at the Church of Everlasting Life, and their meddling. Arrogant idiots. If only they had left well alone. Did you study them in school as well, Paul?'

'Well, not the church people themselves, but in biology our teachers did explain what the church was trying to do, and how it went wrong.'

'Fiddling with nature, weren't they,' said Pierre.

'Yep, they were doing genetic experiments to prevent aging, using a virus to carry the genetic material into humans. Then the virus escaped from the lab and mutated causing the global pandemic, killing billions of people.'

Pierre shook his head.

'I'm sorry for your loss,' said Erin.

'It was a terrible time. But as they say: what doesn't kill you makes you stronger.'

'Were you infected as well?' said Tom.

'Yes.'

'Wow,' said Tom. 'You must have been lucky to survive, with a 95% fatality rate.'

'If you can call it luck, losing my family but surviving myself. I guess that's luck of a sort.'

They drove on in silence. Every few hundred metres Pierre swerved to avoid a pothole.

'I see that they haven't been able to keep up maintenance of this road,' said Erin, 'times must be difficult.'

Pierre laughed.

'This road's always been crap,' he said. 'The contractors pay kickbacks to get the work, then they use substandard materials to increase their profits. So the road is as full of holes as Swiss cheese. Some things never change.'

They travelled through the towns and villages. The fields were well-tended, the houses in good repair and the people well-clothed. In one village they stopped to eat. Pierre insisted, over Erin's protests, on paying for all three of them at a roadside café. They sat outside on aluminium chairs. The bright sun turned the aluminium table top into a mirror, blinding them: Pierre covered it with an old newspaper from the back of the lorry. Tom and Erin had hot croissants, Pierre had frog's legs in olive oil and garlic. Tom watched with a kind of absorbed revulsion as Pierre stuffed the stiff legs in his mouth and chewed. Pierre's jaw moved vigorously up and down and Tom could hear the bones crunch. When he'd finished he let out a loud burp and rubbed his stomach. 'Très bien,' he said. They washed the food down with a carafe of tap water. Refreshed, they jumped back in the cab and drove for a few more hours.

'Where do you want to be dropped?'

'We're meeting Daniel at The Poisson Rouge in Cassis but we don't want you to go out of your way.'

'It's no trouble.'

Towards dusk Pierre stopped the lorry outside the restaurant in Cassis. Judging by the people walking past the window the restaurant was packed. They heard the subdued hubbub of music, laughter and unintelligible chatter.

'Well, here you are,' said Pierre.

'I'll get the bags,' said Tom, climbing out. 'Thanks for the ride, Pierre.'

'Good luck,' said Pierre.

'I can't thank you enough,' said Erin.

'Daniel's not really your cousin, is he?' said Pierre.

Erin looked away avoiding the perceptive brown eyes.

'No.'

'And your name's not Sarah.'

'No. I'm sorry Pierre, I... There are people desperately trying to locate our community in Switzerland.'

'Switzerland? Not the community at An Lac, Annando's place?'

'Yes. They want to destroy it. I thought it better not to use our real names.'

'Well I'll be damned. I've heard of Annando, everybody has. He must be very old now.'

'He is, he's slowing, but catch him at the right time and he still has the mind of a gazelle; he won't retire.'

'I remember people speaking about him. He taught them about global weirding, how to cope and live simply. He helped a lot of people here, he taught them to recycle and think in new ways, and they changed their habits. Destroy your community? Who on earth would want to?'

'The New Islamists.'

'Ah, I understand. That makes sense. Can I do anything for you? I'd be glad to help.'

'No. You've done loads for us already. Just don't mention that you've seen us.'

'Never.'

'My name's Erin,' she said, almost in a whisper.

'Good luck, I'm glad we met. Take care, both of you.'

Erin climbed down and closed the door. Pierre waved and drove off. Tom and Erin went inside 'Le Poisson Rouge'. The air inside was hot and steamy and there was a smell of fresh fish and newly baked bread. A waitress approached them.

'Nous sommes très complet ce soir. Avez vous un reservation?' she said.

'We've come to join a friend of ours. Monsieur Fournier,' said Erin.

'Ah yes, Madame. Let me check for you.' She consulted a list. 'His table is on the veranda, over there.' She pointed to a set of tables ranged down the side of the restaurant facing the quayside. Only one of the tables was occupied by a single diner.

'Merci.'

The man appeared to be in his fifties, with a thatch of greying hair and thick eyebrows to match. His face and neck were tanned and leathery from long exposure to sun and sea.

'Monsieur Fournier?' Erin said. He took a leisurely sip of his beer and looked up at her.

'That is my name,' he said. 'What can I do for you?' His voice was deep and croaky.

'We'd like to hire you and your boat. We want to go fishing.'

'I see, and what do you want to catch?'

'Spanish sardines.'

As Erin spoke M. Fournier noticeably relaxed. He smiled, 'Welcome, I have been waiting here a long time for you. Come and join me, please sit, you must tell me your names.'

Tom and Erin stuffed their rucksacks under the table and sat down. Closer now, Erin could see the collar of his open-neck white shirt was yellow with dirt and grease. He smelled of fish and salt.

'I'm Erin and this is Tom.'

'Very pleased to meet you both. Call me Daniel, please. Would you like something to drink, or to eat, perhaps?' He coughed loudly and cleared his throat.

Tom was about to assent but Erin nudged him with her elbow.

'We're eager to start right away,' she said, 'if that's all right with you.'

'You realise that it may be well after dawn when we get to the fishing grounds? That means that you might miss the opportunity to do your fishing at night.'

'I know, but that can't be helped. We are anxious to get started. If you could get us there before dawn that would be best but if not we'll just have to do it in daylight.'

'I have a fishing boat not a speedboat but I will do what I can. Let's go.' Fournier drained his glass and stood; he was tall, robustly built. He pulled some coins from his pocket and examined them briefly; they clinked as he tossed them onto a small metal plate. Tom and Erin followed him on to the quayside. They walked past vessels of all shapes and sizes until Fournier stopped and waved his arm expansively at a stubby fishing boat.

'There she is.'

'She looks very... sturdy,' said Erin, trying to hide her disappointment.

'She is, she is. Come aboard and make yourselves comfortable.'

That's not likely to happen, thought Erin. The boat wobbled precariously from side to side as they climbed the gangplank. A few steep steps below and they were inside the tiny cabin. Erin found that to her surprise it was very cosy, like an intimate hotel bar. Red velvet sofas faced each other; there were wood panels and a green carpet. Colourful mugs hung from hooks in neat rows, two smoky glass table lamps gave a subdued glow. There was that distinct fishy, salty smell.

Fournier produced a simple meal of bread, cheese, grapes and almonds that Erin and Tom devoured while he got the boat underway. Once they had cleared the harbour, Erin went on deck and stood beside him; she breathed in the sea air. The night was clear, the stars tiny pinpricks of light all over the sky. The lights of the harbour glowed brightly behind the black silhouettes of the boats.

'Now, where exactly am I taking you?'

'Cabo de Creus please.'

'The peninsula. I know it well. I'll take you as close as I can.'

'Thank you. It's a fine night; how long will it take to get there?'

'Probably five to six hours depending on conditions. I should get you there about eight o'clock in the morning.'

'Can you get us there before dawn?'

'If it stays like this we should make good time. I can't promise to get you there before sunup though.'

'We cannot afford to delay until the next night. We have to get to Madrid as soon as we possibly can.'

'You and Tom should get some sleep. It'll be a long night and you'll have a difficult journey across Spain to Madrid.'

'Do you know what conditions are like there now?'

'Not good.'

'That's what I thought. Can I just check something with you; I've heard that English is the spoken language in Spain now.'

'That's right. There were so many immigrants they needed a common language; most people speak English.'

'Thanks.'

Erin went below. Tom was already in his sleeping bag spread out on one of the red sofas. She climbed into hers.

'Goodnight, Aunt Sarah.'

'I hate it when you call me that.'

'I know.' Tom grinned and closed his eyes.

*

Erin woke to the smell of fresh coffee.

'That smells good,' she said.

'Drink it quickly,' said Fournier. 'It's almost time for you to go.' He coughed.

'You need that cough seen to,' said Erin.

'It's only an old smoker's cough, nothing. Anyway, there aren't many doctors around nowadays. Stay fit and healthy if you can.'

Erin gulped her hot coffee. A plate of bread rolls was laid out on the galley table. She ate two, still warm.

'Where's Tom? He should have something as well before we leave.'

'Tom's already eaten. He's on deck looking for the lights of any other boats that may spot us.'

'Looking for lights? Then that means... '

'Yes, there's still an hour before dawn.'

'That's a miracle! You're fantastic, Daniel!'

'Luckily there was a fast current going our way. Helped us along.'

'Don't be modest.'

61

Daniel shrugged. 'Anyway, time to get you two ashore. We're about half a mile north of Cabo de Creus. I'll lower the dinghy. I can row you further in, to within a few hundred metres of the beach. You'll have to wade the final part but it should be only knee-deep. Get your stuff together while I get the dinghy; I'll send Tom down to help you.'

'Thanks, Daniel, it'll only take a few minutes to get ready.'

A short while later Tom and Erin stepped out of the dinghy into the sea. Daniel was right, it came up only to their knees.

'Thanks for the ride, and the food,' said Tom, striding towards the shore.

'Safe journey, Daniel, and look after that cough,' said Erin. 'We may have need of a lift home. Would that be possible? To pick us up from here and take us back to Cassis?'

'Sure. Just send a message through the network, with the date and time when you need to be collected. I'll come and fetch you.'

'There would probably be three of us.'

'No problem.'

'Daniel, I can't thank you enough for all your help.'

'No thanks needed. Now be off with you before the sun comes up.'

There was already a definite lightening of the sky towards the east.

Erin shook his rough dry hand and hurried to catch up with Tom. She could see his figure moving like a smudge, dark and ghostly, nearly ashore. The sea was almost flat and reflected the moonlight like a mirror; the waves lapped gently on the sand. Erin stepped out of the surf and clambered up the beach; her wet trousers clung to her legs. Tom was seated on a large slab of flat rock, waiting.

'There's a small clump of bushes over there,' he said, pointing. 'We could hide there while we get our bearings.'

'Good idea, Tom. Let's go.'

Once among the bushes Erin shone her torch at the map.

'I reckon we're a couple of kilometres outside Rosas,' she said. 'If we strike inland we should see it soon. Then we just have to skirt the town to the other side and locate the café.'

'We've just eaten, but OK, I'm up for it.'

Erin gave Tom a withering look.

'If that's meant to be a joke, it's not very funny, Tom.'

'Sorry. Oh, am I Paul today, and you Aunt Sarah?'

'You're pushing your luck, TOM. No, we'll use our real names with this contact. He already knows to expect Erin and Tom, anyway.'

'Why are they always men, our contacts? It wouldn't hurt to be picked up by a choice chick for a change.'

Erin sighed. 'Tom, keep it holstered. Choice chick? Is that what you youngsters call an attractive young woman these days? As it happens, nondescript men attract much less attention than "choice chicks" do, as you so colourfully put it. We're trying to stay inconspicuous, remember?'

'I'm only saying.'

'Yes, well don't say. Walk.'

As they left the shade of the bushes, the sun was now above the horizon, the air was already warmer. Erin felt the warm air dry her trousers; it was going to be a hot day. She led the way across the stark terrain. Sand was mixed in with dirt, a few shrubs and cacti pushed through the soil. They could see the town of Rosas on the horizon and gave it a wide berth. On the trail the only signs of life were colourful lizards scuttling in the sparse undergrowth, their tails rustling. Half an hour's brisk walking brought them to a dilapidated building just off the dusty track. It had a corrugated iron roof painted brilliant white to reflect the sun's heat. Looking at it was almost blinding in the full sun. Two plastic chairs and a battered wooden table stood on the dirty forecourt along with two cars and a pickup truck. In the doorway hung a tatty green PVC strip curtain, faded by the sun. Erin could hear men with hard voices talking inside. Swinging from a wrought iron frame was a large board with 'Los Antilos', written in red Gothic script.

'This is the place,' said Erin.

A few yards away a dark, black-haired man was sitting on the ground, propped against the trunk of a tree. He was wearing mirrored sunglasses and had a can of beer in his hand.

'Wait here,' Erin took a deep breath. 'Excuse me, do you know the way to Buenos Aires?'

'No, but I know the way to Madrid.' He stood and took off his sunglasses, his piercing blue eyes contrasting with the dark of his skin. He was well over six feet tall and one of the most handsome men she had ever seen. To her surprise and consternation some indescribable sensation inside her was roused; she bit her lip and pushed the feeling away.

'You must be Erin, my name is Leon Ricardo Sanz,' he said in English with a heavy Spanish accent. 'But please, call me Leon.' He took her hand and gave it a firm squeeze. A tingling sensation rose up her arm. She stifled it. Erin turned to indicate Tom.

'This is Tom, my travelling companion.'

'Pleased to meet you, Tom,' said Leon, shaking his hand.

'Hi,' said Tom. Nondescript my foot, he thought.

'Come,' said Leon, as he led them over to the pickup truck. He flung open the passenger door. A shotgun lay on the seat.

'Do you always travel with this?' asked Erin.

'I've been ambushed a few times. They try to steal the truck. You can never be too careful.' Leon picked up the shotgun and placed it on hooks fixed to the back panel above the seat. The air inside the cabin was like a furnace.

Erin could feel the heat from the leather seat through her thin trousers almost burning her skin. Patches of yellow foam poked through the torn leather. The windows were grimy and there was a faint odour of sweat and aftershave. As Leon turned the engine there was a loud abrasive noise. The truck started to vibrate, slowly and regularly. Leon drove out of the forecourt and on to the open road. When he pressed down on the accelerator, a juddering pulsed through them. Each time he changed gear the truck laboured and screeched. Tom felt all his nerves were on edge. Erin was suffering as well but was determined to silently put up with it, partly to set an example to Tom and, well, because there was something about Leon.

'I've got a headache,' said Tom after about an hour.

Erin passed him a bottle of water.

'Here, drink this it should help,' she said sternly. Tom had hoped for some sympathy but he was evidently not going to get any. For the first time he began to think it may have been a mistake to come on this journey, but it was obviously far too late for second thoughts.

Soon the road started to climb as they got nearer to the hills. The truck's vibrations lessened and the grating noise stopped. Tom's headache eased. As they climbed higher the air became cooler. Shortly after midday they crested the hill and started to descend. Leon stopped the truck on a level patch of ground beside the road.

'Time to eat and rest,' he said. He pointed to a cluster of small boulders. 'Sit over there and I'll bring you food.'

Tom and Erin stretched then settled themselves on the flattest boulders they could find. Erin watched as Leon lifted a large coolbox out of the back of the pickup truck and carried it towards them; she noticed the lithe and nimble way he moved.

65

'This is really unexpected,' said Erin, 'and kind of you.'

'You're welcome. Are you ready to eat?'

Tom licked his lips.

'There are two things,' said Erin, 'that Tom is ready to do at any time, anywhere. One of them is eat.'

Leon chuckled. Tom reddened and frowned.

'I'm hungry as well,' said Erin.

Tom noticed some subtle change in Erin's body language, something he'd never seen before. He was disgusted that Erin could be so easily impressed. Erin was just Erin, hard and impenetrable, rational through and through, or so he thought. He relied on that, she was his rock.

'Good. Well, help yourselves.' Leon opened the coolbox and pushed it towards them. Tom picked up an odd-looking roll, shaped like a dog's bone and cut through the middle, it felt cool and soft to the touch.

'I haven't seen these before. What are these called,' asked Tom.

'Boccadillos,' said Leon proudly. 'I made them myself.'

'That's very clever of you,' said Erin.

What a stupid thing for Erin to say, Tom thought. He cringed.

Tom raised the roll to his mouth, but Erin put up her hand.

'Wait, Tom,' she said. 'Leon, you do know we're vegetarian, don't you?'

'Yes, there's no meat in the food at all.' Tom took a bite.

'Just ham,' said Leon. Tom spat it out.

'Leon,' said Erin, gently, 'for us ham is meat as well.'

'Really? That's crazy.'

'Yes, really.'

'Well I'm sorry, I didn't know. No-one thinks ham is meat.'

'That's all right. It was very good of you to take the trouble to make a picnic for us. And we can take the ham out and eat the rest, can't we Tom?' Tom had already removed the slice of ham and wolfed down the rest.

'Are we going to stay in Madrid? asked Erin.

'Yes, there's a safe house... belongs to a man called Aziz. He's a good man and he'll feed you well.'

'How long will it take to get to Madrid from here?' said Tom as they pulled off down the road.

'Hard to say, it depends on the road, the other traffic, with luck we'll be there in another six hours or so. Roads are good up here but once we get close to Madrid it will get worse.'

'Why's that?' Erin deftly pushed her hair behind her ears.

'The northern part of Spain is mostly the same so far. But the south is swarming with refugees and the New Islamists have taken over. Our way of life has mostly fallen apart. New Islam is spreading northwards all the time, but you must know this.'

'Yes.'

'Now it's reached Madrid, and in fact areas north of Madrid as well. I reckon that at this rate it'll only be a year or so before all of Spain is like that.'

'Unless someone can stop it,' said Erin.

'Like who? Superman? I don't think it can be stopped,' said Leon.

'There's always hope,' said Erin.

'Maybe,' said Leon.

Close to Madrid, Erin and Tom could see that Leon had not exaggerated. The road which was well-maintained up to this point was studded with potholes. Leon tried his best to miss them, but many were unavoidable, and they lurched from side to side in the truck as it bumped its way through them. It was late afternoon now and the scorching heat of the middle of the day was gone, but it was still uncomfortably warm. Fields stretched out on both sides of the road, with scores of people busily collecting the harvest. In one field black-clad women with bent backs were collecting potatoes, tossing them into large baskets strapped on their backs. In another field men were using scythes to cut down wheat.

'What's that?' asked Tom, pointing at a device made of long poles, ropes and a bucket. 'It looks medieval to me. Don't they have modern machines?'

'That's a shadouf,' said Leon. 'It has been used in the Middle East for thousands of years to lift water from irrigation ditches to water the crops in the field. Now they are being used here because fuel for engines is scarce and expensive. The shadouf can be operated by a man and manual labour is cheap and readily available.'

'I hope the Muslims treat them well,' said Erin, 'working in this heat could kill you.'

'They choose the strong healthy ones for this work. Any that fall ill are quickly replaced. There are always plenty of new recruits,' said Leon.

Tom sat in silence. Erin turned and glanced at him. He had pushed himself into the corner, his face deathly pale.

At the outskirts of Madrid a city of green tents appeared on the horizon. Row upon row stood like dismal markers in the smoggy air. There was a smell that Erin couldn't identify: it was akin to rotting fish. They passed two corpses by the side of the road.

'They'll be collected later. The authorities come by once a day. There's a big burial pit some way out of town.'

Shelters with walls made from polythene bags and roofs beaten from diesel drums appeared at the side of the road, increasing in frequency as the truck moved on.

Destitute people dressed in rags milled about the pavements aimlessly, spilling into the road. Bedraggled children queued miserably with plastic containers, waiting to use a solitary standpipe. They passed a building set back from the road. It had a large billboard outside, with 'Universidad de Vida Simple' written on it in bold black capital letters.

'What's that place?' asked Tom.

'University of Simple Living; they issue Diplomas there,' said Leon.

'What do they teach?' asked Erin.

'Resources, natural disasters, recycling and also about Islam. Their own version of it anyway. They don't tell you that last bit though if you're a refugee. You can get time off to attend, rather than toiling in the fields. It's very popular because of that of course.'

They passed another building; the sign outside said 'Centro Medico'. There was a queue at the entrance that stretched round the whole building and out of sight.

'Not much good if you're seriously ill,' said Erin dismally, 'you'd be dead before you got to the front of the queue!'

'They have scouts who go up and down the queue, spotting the most seriously ill. Mostly they're the ones who are lying down or being carried by someone else. If they're lucky they'll get taken in and treated.'

'I feel sick,' said Tom.

'Tom, notice and move on,' said Erin, 'focus on our mission, only on that.'

Erin and Leon both looked at him. Tom could see his own reflection in Leon's mirrored sunglasses, tucked in a corner with his arms around his knees. Tom took a deep breath and stretched himself upright.

'I'll be OK,' he said.

CHAPTER 7

An Lac ashram, Switzerland

'Ah, there you are.' Ralph clambered down the grassy bank. 'I got your message; it sounded like it couldn't wait, what is it?'

'Ralph, I need to talk with you,' said Stefano.

'Sure, how can I help?'

'In here.'

Ralph followed him into the large airy barn lined with straw that smelt of animals and dung. Chickens milled around restlessly squawking and flapping their wings.

'There are so many of them, but I know each one.' Stefano's deep voice sounded soft and affectionate. He dug into his pocket, pulled out some grain and scattered it on the ground. The chickens pecked at it.

'You're fond of them,' said Ralph.

'I am... Ralph, what's going on?'

'What do you mean?'

'Annando's asked me to go to Turkey with Ajit, as his travelling companion.' Stefano stared gravely and intensely at Ralph. 'Some meeting or other with an imam. Annando did explain and I said I understood at the time but I've been mulling it over... help me, will you. What's it all about?'

'It's a diplomatic mission. Annando has contacts who know the imam. He's called Jalal Kowi. He's not like most of the others, he's learned, more moderate, a man of principles and not easily corrupted. Annando wants to make contact with him, to get his cooperation.'

'His cooperation? With what?'

'Annando said our message must be for everyone, and that includes the New Islamists as well. He's hoping that Jalal Kowi will be useful in helping us to reach out to them.

So Annando has arranged for Ajit to meet Jalal Kowi in the desert, in Turkey. He's sending Ajit because they're both academic men, which might help them understand each other. He told me you'd agreed to go, to give Ajit support.'

'I did.' Stefano scratched his scalp. 'As you know Annando is a difficult man to say no to. But I don't think I'm the right person.' He looked quickly at Ralph, then away again.

'Why not?'

'You know me; I haven't left the ashram for twelve years. I won't know how to get there and I don't speak the language.'

'That's not quite true; you do the local run into the village.'

'But that's all, Ralph, that's all.'

'Annando always makes considered decisions; you know that. He must have chosen you for good reasons.'

'He said he wanted to give me a challenge, stop me stagnating, help me become more confident. But I'm not inert here, I've got a lot of responsibility.' Stefano frowned. 'What do you think he meant?'

'That's private between you and Annando.'

'Of course I love and respect Annando, we all do but... '

'Annando will challenge us all... it's part of our spiritual development.'

Stefano walked to a trough, stooped down, shoved his hand deep inside and filled his pockets with more grain; some spilled on the ground. Ralph followed and stood next to him; he felt the small hard grains under the soles of his shoes.

'This feed is for the girls in the other barn.' Stefano turned his back on Ralph.

'Look, you won't have to make any arrangements, that's all done for you by our contacts. And you know almost

71

everyone speaks English now, even in the desert, so it won't be that difficult.'

Stefano flung some grain across the barn and the chickens clustered around squawking in a feeding frenzy. He glanced at Ralph and shook his head.

'Why don't you go instead?'

'I would, I've offered but Annando wants me here running things.'

'Not good for me then... Do me a favour will you, Ralph?' Ralph saw Stefano's eyes fearful. 'Tell Annando to choose someone else.'

'You need to talk to him yourself.'

'If I go I might mess up and I don't want to let anyone down.'

Ralph stepped back.

'There's no reason why you should, just do your best. You're more able than you think, you can do this,' said Ralph as he walked out.

Looking back he saw Stefano had picked up a chicken and tucked it under his arm, stroking it absently.

CHAPTER 8

Madrid, Spain

Tom handed the grim official his meal ticket and joined the queue that snaked around the building towards the canteen. The refugees were quiet and sombre waiting patiently as the line jerked slowly forwards. Most women were dressed the same in black chador with a few in casual clothes. They're probably newcomers, Tom thought. There were so many people, nobody had noticed him, he'd just merged into the crowd. He was pleased with himself for duping the authorities and felt only a smidgen of trepidation. Once inside the air was steamy and saturated with a smell of potatoes and soggy cabbage. The clatter of metal cutlery echoed around the prefabricated walls that were yellow and grimy with contact from so many sweaty bodies. The roof was low and made of corrugated iron. Tom reached the buffet. Three sullen women in black stood behind huge pots of food. He remembered his father saying 'when in Rome do as the Romans do' so he did exactly as the man in front. He took a battered wooden tray and a dented metallic plate from a pile. The plate was cold to the touch and slightly greasy.

One of the three women called, 'Next.'

She ladled a steaming brownish semi-liquid substance that smelt of cabbage and spice onto his plate. The next woman put on a cube of black bread and the third a spoonful of yoghurt. Plastic cups of water were laid out in rows; some were pitted, another had teeth marks around the edge. He winced, chose the most unblemished and put it on his tray. He picked up a bent knife, a fork and a paper napkin so thin and small it looked like a single piece of toilet paper, from the end of the buffet. This is the pits, what disgusting food, thought Tom. He compared it to the colourful vegetables and delicious smell of fresh bread that used to make his taste buds run wild at An Lac. He looked around for somewhere to sit. There were rows and rows of wooden tables with benches, men on one side of the hall, women on the other. He'd never seen so many people eating together. A few groups were talking quietly. He noticed the people had strangely bland expressions with staring eyes. Tom found an empty spot at a table. As he sat down the men looked up at him indifferently; the man opposite scooped up spoonfuls of the mixture and slurped it down.

'What do you think this is?' said Tom.

He stirred the strange unappetising concoction with his fork. Pink globules were mixed in. He grimaced.

The man opposite stopped slurping. 'Difficult to tell, I think it's beef stew,' he said in a deep voice and slurped again. He looked better dressed than the others. His black hair was combed back, his features strong and he had a profusion of nostril hair; his eyes were bright and alert.

'Yuck, I'm a vegetarian,' said Tom, 'I don't want to eat this.'

'This is the only food, it's this or nothing,' said a man in a grimy overall on his right in a matter of fact way.

The man opposite studied him.

'I think I'll get some different food somewhere else,' said Tom, 'but I'll eat the bread.' He bit off a fragment of the dark coloured bread and chewed it. It was tough and tasted of charcoal.

The man on his right frowned. 'You need to take the charity that's offered. It's not for you to question it.'

'I'm not questioning it for others,' said Tom, 'but I have decided that meat eating is not for me. Why should I have to?'

The man opposite continued looking at Tom whilst he slowly and carefully sipped his water. Finished, he stared

Tom straight in the eye, 'This is the kind of dangerous and egocentric thinking that brought about the downfall of moral values and the destruction of the planet. People need strong leadership and guidance to become good Muslims.'

Tom was vaguely aware that the man on his left had his head down and he heard the rustle of paper.

'But you need to find the guidance inside you,' said Tom.

'How is that?' asked the man opposite.

'By meditation, by going within. Everyone can do it. There's no point in praying five times a day as a ritual if you're not going to be transformed. Habits without a meaning just turn you into an automaton. Where I come from we're transformed from inside. Life-giving choices come from inside, because we're in touch with the source of life beyond doctrine.'

'You must become a Muslim if you want to be saved,' said the man on his right coldly.

'What, saved after death?' asked Tom.

'Before and after death, yes.'

'Being saved after death is just an idea of the imagination; none of us are dead yet, so we don't know. But I'm sure saying a few words in front of two witnesses and becoming a Muslim isn't going to save you.'

Tom looked at his cup of water. He was thirsty but it had a greasy film floating on top and smelt of chlorine. He took a sip: it was tepid and tasted metallic.

'I can see you need help understanding,' said the man opposite with narrowed eyes.

'I don't need any help; maybe you need to meditate.'

Abruptly Tom felt his elbow being shoved from the left and heard the clanging of metal cutlery; he grabbed the table to stop falling over. 'Your fork has fallen on the floor,' the man on his left said firmly, 'you need to pick it up.'

Tom leant backwards leaving some room between him and the table and looked down. A piece of paper was laid out over the legs of the man on his left. Scribbled on it in large letters was the message: 'DANGER! GET OUT'. Tom froze, he felt his heart thump. Slowly he collected the fork from the floor and placed it on the table; the man on his left was looking away. Tom's mind raced. He swallowed hard, took a deep breath and stood up.

'Where are you going?' said the man opposite.

'To the toilet.'

'I'll come with you, and then we'll continue our little chat.' There was something cold and clinical in the man's expression and tone of voice that made Tom's blood run cold. Tom walked abruptly to the back of the hall and followed the signs to the toilet, aware of the oppressive presence of the man close behind. There were two single cubicles. Tom dived into one of them and locked the door.

'Fuck, fuck,' he said under his breath, trembling. It was a tiny space and there was a strong smell of urine mixed with disinfectant with one small window in the wall above the toilet. He unfastened the handle and the window swung round 180 degrees on two horizontal central pivot hinges. Tom fished his Swiss army knife out of his back pocket, selected the screwdriver and with feverish hands undid the screws at the top of the window. It quickly loosened. He heard a man urinating and the loud flush of the toilet next door. With one hand holding the top in place he used the other to unscrew the bottom hinge.

There was a knock on the door. The man said in a firm voice, 'Are you ready?'

'Just coming,' said Tom.

He flushed the toilet to muffle the sound, with brute force yanked the pivot window from the frame and flung it out of the hole. 'Fuck,' he said. He felt beads of sweat on his forehead, his heart thumped. He stood on the toilet and pushed his arms through the hole grabbing the outer window frame and forcing his shoulders and chest through the tiny space. He ignored the blistering pain on his chest and ribs as his skin rubbed against the sharp wood. He needed to get OUT, OUT, OUT. He was half in and half out. In front of him was a rubbish-filled alleyway that smelt of dustbins. He pushed with his arms against the outside wall and his hips came through the opening. He crashed heavily on the dirty ground with his arms breaking his fall. Shaking, he got to his feet and sprinted away. Once the canteen was out of sight he leant up against a wall, panting heavily. He stopped and looked briefly down at himself; his clothes were torn and blood seeped through from scratches and abrasions. He grimaced in pain, and ran on. He was driven, with only one goal in mind, to get back to Erin and safety.

*

Erin's expression was stern but her touch was tender. He winced.

'Ow, that hurts,' he said as she bathed the cuts and grazes on his shoulder.

'They will, they're nasty wounds, gone quite deep into the skin.'

He studied her. 'You're angry, aren't you?'

'Yes, but you're back now. Relief is my overriding feeling. I expect I'll get angry later. It was a bloody stupid thing to do.' She took the cloth and rinsed it in the bowl of water. They were silent for a moment. 'Tell me about the people in the canteen.'

'They looked strange.'

'In what way?'

'Their faces were staring, like zombies, as if they'd been drugged. I've never seen people like that before.' Tom shivered. 'I can't imagine what it must be like to be told what to think and what to do, or even not think for yourself at all. I suppose that's the way I might have become after they'd 'educated' me.'

'I don't think so, you'd become like the guy sitting next to you, quietly rebelling, or you'd be locked up permanently, like Carlos.'

'I never realised how lucky I was living in the ashram, always able to say how I felt, to be free to have my own thoughts and ideas. It must be terrible for these people.'

'I guess it's similar to institutionalisation.'

'What's that?'

'In the Victorian era people were locked away in institutions for all kind of reasons; some had mental health problems, some were single women who were pregnant. After some time they found these people all had the same syndrome. Their choices had been taken away and they couldn't think for themselves anymore. They lost their individuality and initiative. They became dependent and needed to be told what to do. It's a sorry state to be in and very difficult to reverse.'

Tom was pensive for a moment. 'God, I could have been locked away. That would have been terrible. You'd have had to help me escape as well.'

'Well, it hasn't happened, thankfully.'

'I can't bear Annando thinking badly of me. I don't want to let Dad down,' said Tom thoughtfully, 'even worse than that, I don't want to let Annando down.'

'Why is letting Annando down worse?'

'Dad judges me and Annando doesn't. He forgives everybody, doesn't he?'

'Only when they're learning,' said Erin quietly.

Tom shivered suddenly.

'Are you cold?'

'Yes.'

She put a blanket round him. His face looked deathly white.

'You've had a scare,' said Erin.

'Yeah.'

'It's a steep learning curve for you.'

'But I'm learning.'

'Maybe not quickly enough,' said Erin.

'But I'll show you. I can learn fast. I'm even more determined to get Carlos out now.'

Erin said, 'Hmmm, I'm not so sure about that.'

Tom frowned and raised his voice. 'You're not going to dump me, you can't. Not for one little mistake.'

Erin looked at him and said nothing.

'I'll show you I can do it. I won't let you down.'

CHAPTER 9

'Erin, it'll be all right, honestly, I'll be very careful, I promise.' Tom scraped the last of the yoghurt out of the bowl, licked it off the spoon, sat back and rubbed his stomach. 'Yum.'

Erin frowned. 'After your last little escapade in that canteen I'm not sure. Can I trust you not to get into trouble?' She cupped her hands round her mug of coffee, feeling the warmth spreading along her fingers.

'Oh, come on,' said Tom.

'You nearly got yourself hauled off to who knows where, and endangered the whole mission. You could have compromised An Lac itself. Once they realize that you're one of the community, you've had it. Believe me, when they start questioning you they'll wheedle it all out of you. They're experts at interrogation and I hate to think what else they'd do to you. Before you know it you'll find you've told them everything.'

'I'll be very careful. Just a little look round, see the lay of the land. We can't go in there blind, can we? Not if we're to get Carlos out.'

'No, we certainly need more information than we have now. That's what I hope we'll get from Aziz, and maybe Raphael.'

'I still think it would help if I had a look at the place before we go in, then it won't be new to me during the raid. I'll be very careful, really I will.'

'Well, I suppose it would be useful for you to see what it's like.' Erin sighed and pushed her hair behind her ears. 'Do you know what you're looking for?'

'Yes, a two storey red brick building with bars at the windows.'

'But you're not to go in, do you hear? Under no circumstances are you to enter the building. On pain of death.'

'What, they're not going to kill me just for walking in, are they?'

'No, but I will', muttered Erin.

'Ha ha,' said Tom, weakly. 'Very funny.'

'Yes, well I'm obviously not really going to kill you. But I'll make it so you'll wish I had.' Erin scrutinised him like a mother hen. 'Be off with you, and make sure you don't cause any more mischief.'

Tom grinned, abruptly got up and strode out of the room.

*

Tom made his way past Los Rosales and Villaverde to the south side of Madrid. A few streets away a tall glass and concrete building dominated the skyline. He crossed an empty dual carriageway. It was clear he was not in the residential part of the city; there were a few scattered shops and small cafés with customers inside interspersed amongst buildings which appeared to be mainly offices. Some had missing or boarded-up windows, others were splattered with red and black graffiti. A tattered billboard bore the faded words: 'Bienvenidos al distrito de negocios de Madrid'. Not much of a business district now, thought Tom. The warm air hovered round the buildings, Tom felt the heat of the paving stones coming through the soles of his shoes. He caught the whiff of something rotting somewhere. Sweat trickled down the back of his neck and under his shirt; he felt the fabric stick to his back. A sudden gust of wind whipped around the corner of a building. A ball of paper whacked against a metal doorway and twittered away along the pavement; an empty tin can clattered as it was swept along. Dust swirled in the air, making his eyes smart. Turning left he heard the

81

echo of angry male voices; he stopped for a moment and listened. A man coughed, someone else let out a long painful groan. As he turned another corner he saw the detention centre standing imposingly on a street corner about thirty metres away. Tom looked quickly in all directions; he felt like a rat in the wrong place. With a bang the front door swung open and two men in uniform came thumping down the front steps. Tom felt his heart pound almost in time with the officers' boots on concrete; they strode confidently down the street, glancing indifferently at him. Tom crossed the road and round the corner of a building. There was a narrow alleyway behind. As he walked on he heard light female voices. Ahead was a tight group of three young women standing in the shade a few metres inside the passageway. They were all dressed head to foot in black, their faces uncovered. One was fanning herself with what looked like a copy of the official local newspaper. Catching sight of Tom she leaned forward to say something to the others. All three looked at him and giggled. Tom stopped. He could see clearly now they were Caucasian, wearing their garments awkwardly. It seemed forever since he'd had the opportunity to spend some time with any women closer to his own age than Erin.

'Hi,' he said. 'I seem to have lost my way. Do you know where Playa Major is?'

'You know we're not supposed to speak to any male who isn't a relative. How do we know you're not here to get us into trouble? Tricking us and then turning us over to the authorities.'

Her voice was coarse and loud, she had wisps of blonde hair pushing out from under her hijab. He took a few steps forward and caught a scent of perfume. His pulse quickened.

'For all they know, I could be your long-lost cousin,' he said. 'My name's Tom by the way. Cousin Tom from out of town.'

'Chloe,' said the blonde. She pulled up her sleeves and exposed her white arms covered in colourful bangles and tattoos. The bangles jangled as she gyrated to noiseless music. 'And all my cousins are as ugly as sin. I wish they were out of town.' She raised her arms in the air and did a full turn. The fabric of her chador swirled. He felt hot air currents move. 'I'd swap them for you any day.' She came to a stop and looked appraisingly at him, her gaze lingering on his face as she lightly licked her lips. Tom swallowed hard. 'This is Anna,' she said, indicating the woman on her left. 'And that's Odette over there.' She waved her hand vaguely in Odette's direction. Odette's gown was hitched up. She had thin dainty ankles and wore strappy leather sandals.

'Hello, Anna,' said Tom, turning to face her. 'And are you blonde as well?'

Tom took one cautious pace forward; the girls giggled. He detected something wild and reckless in Anna's eyes that put him on his guard. Anna reached up and slowly and deliberately removed her hijab. With the movement her chador tightened across her chest, revealing the shape of her breasts thrusting against the fabric. She shook out her long mousy brown hair and gazed feverishly at him. Tom struggled to tear his eyes away from Anna's luscious breasts. He felt himself harden. Looking down Anna eyed the bulge in his trousers and grinned. 'Seen something you like?' she purred. Tom blushed.

'You're all too fit to be covered in this garb,' he said, trying to sound cool. 'Why do you wear it?'

'If we don't, we don't eat,' said Odette in a matter of fact way. Her voice was soft and clear.

'So they make you hide yourselves away. What a waste.'

'But these clothes can come off quite easily, in the right circumstances,' said Chloe. 'Like this.'

Chloe lifted her skirt above her waist, revealing bare legs and very skimpy briefs. Tom swallowed hard. He was now definitely out of his depth. As she let the skirt drop she laughed hilariously.

Tom took a closer look at Odette - she was very plain - and turned to her. 'Do you three spend a lot of time lurking in alleyways?'

'Don't be cheeky. I'm waiting for my father, he'll finish work and be here any minute. Chloe and Anna are just keeping me company while I wait.'

'Do you meet him here every day?'

'No, just sometimes.' Odette looked round. 'Oh look, there he is now. We must go. Bye.' The three women dashed off. Tom felt his shirt sticky on his chest as he sweated; every cell in his body was on fire. He didn't quite know what to make of it, but he knew he felt good.

*

'Well,' said Erin, as Tom settled himself in the armchair 'Was it a useful visit?'

Tom grinned widely. 'Very useful.'

'Oh no, you look too pleased with yourself for it to have been just a look at the detention centre. What else have you been up to?'

'Nothing, Erin.'

'Come on, Tom, I know you better than that. Spill it.'

'Well, I did meet some girls.'

'I knew it. Do you ever think about anything besides sex?'

'Sometimes.'

'Not often though. Who are these girls? I hope you didn't give anything away.'

There was a soft click from the door, Aziz came in and sat on the sofa next to Erin. 'Hello, Tom.'

'Tom's debriefing me,' said Erin.

'I was very careful: I didn't tell them anything. Anyway they were only there for a few minutes. Two of them were keeping the third one company while she waited for her father to finish work and meet her.'

'You were outside the prison?' said Aziz.

'Yes.'

'Did you speak to the father?' said Erin.

'No, Odette spotted him in the distance and they ran off to meet him. I didn't even see him.'

'Did you say the daughter was called Odette?' Aziz asked.

'Yes, why?'

'Well, you know that I've been keeping watch on the centre trying to get as much information as I can?'

Tom nodded.

'One of the staff has a daughter who often comes there. I've heard him call her Odette. Did this girl's father come out of the centre?'

'I don't know. As I said I didn't see him myself.'

'Odette is not a common name in Spain,' said Aziz. 'It must be the same girl. That's very interesting.'

'Perhaps we can get some useful information out of her about the inside of the detention centre,' ventured Tom.

'And perhaps she'll tell her father all about us,' said Erin.

'She doesn't know anything about us so far.'

'It's too risky, Tom,' Erin shook her head. 'Leave her well alone. What are you planning to do, anyway? Flatter her and wait for her to fall into your arms?'

'Not exactly, but I think that she may be susceptible, because of her friends.'

'What on earth do you mean?' Erin frowned.

'Well the other two, Chloe and Anna...'

'You said they were only there a few minutes, and you got all their names?'

'That's the point. The other two are very forward, very sexy, in fact.' His lip curled into a smile, 'Odette is... different. She's quieter and plain-looking. I would think that when the three of them meet blokes, that she always gets overlooked. I reckon she will be vulnerable. I should be able to work on that, flatter her and pay her compliments and such. She'll fall for it, I'm sure.' Tom glanced at Erin. 'What, why are you looking at me like that?'

Erin took a deep breath. 'Tom, when I was thinking about whether to bring you on this mission, I expected that on this journey you would change and develop. That you would grow up, in fact. You are growing up. You have changed. I'm not sure that I like how you're changing, though. You're set on exploiting a vulnerable human being for your own selfish ends.'

'It's not selfish! It's to get Carlos out of detention. It's not for me. I'm doing it for Carlos, and you, and Annando and the mission.'

'Nevertheless, it's not right.'

'Well, can you think of a better way to get the information we need?'

'No, dammit I can't!' shouted Erin. 'But I don't bloody like it!'

*

Tom walked briskly looking straight ahead, he rounded the corner of the detention centre and stopped at the entrance to the alleyway. There was a girl in black leaning against a concrete whitewashed wall; he recognised the short chador, thin ankles and strappy sandals. Odette was absorbed in a book; looking around there was no sign of Chloe or Anna.

Perhaps the first step would be easier than he had expected: he would not have to think up some ploy to get Odette on her own. As she looked up and saw him her face broke into an excited smile, her small even teeth tinged yellow.

'Hello,' she said. 'Did you find it all right?'

Tom frowned, puzzled. 'Find what?'

'The Playa Major.'

'Oh, that.' He remembered now, he had been pretending to look for the Playa Major as a ploy to speak to the girls.

'Er…' he began.

'You weren't really looking for it, were you?'

Tom smiled, sheepishly. 'No, you've got me, that was just an excuse to talk to you all.'

'Well, you're out of luck today, there's just me.'

'That suits me fine.'

'I don't believe you, blokes prefer them.'

'Chloe and Anna are fit, it's true. But they're both a bit... flashy.'

Odette frowned. 'Yes they are,' she said. 'But that's what men want, isn't it?'

'Not all of us.'

'I'm in luck for once then.' Her face broke into a coy smile.

'Actually, I came here today hoping that you would be here. I've thought about you a lot since we met yesterday. I'd like to spend some time with you. Can we go for a walk or something?'

She tilted her head to one side, studied him for a moment and giggled.

'Sure. We'll have to be discreet though, Cousin Tom.'

She bent down and shoved her book into a satchel at her feet, lifted the bag and swung the strap over her shoulder, staggering a little.

'That looks heavy. Why don't you let me carry it for you?'

'That's very chivalrous of you, Tom, but I can manage, thanks.'

'No, please let me.'

'Well, just for a while then.' She handed the satchel to Tom. He passed the strap over his head and let the bag hang at his hip.

'Where can we go?' asked Tom.

'I know a secluded place, the girls and I sometimes go there to get away from it all.'

'Are they likely to be there now?'

'God, no. They only go there when they're with me.'

'Shouldn't that be "Allah, no"?'

'That's not funny, Tom.'

'Sorry.'

Odette guided Tom through a maze of side streets. He soon gave up trying to keep track of their route; he was totally lost. After ten minutes, Odette led Tom down a walkway between two tall wooden fences.

'Here we are.' She stopped in front of a gate fastened with a sturdy padlock with a combination lock.

'Don't tell me,' said Tom, 'you just happen to know the combination.'

'No, it's better than that.' She yanked the padlock and the clasp emerged and swung free. Pushing the gate open she gestured for Tom to go inside.

'That's amazing,' he said. 'It wasn't locked at all. Anyone can get in.'

'But they don't. They see what they expect to see, a locked gate. So they're locked out as effectively as if the padlock was working.'

'How did you ever find this place, and the secret of the lock?'

'A friend of Anna's, Julio, showed us. He never did say how he knew. Every time we asked him he just smirked. That was a while ago: he disappeared sometime last year.

No-one knows what happened to him, perhaps he left the country, perhaps he upset someone in power and now he's locked up somewhere. Or dead.'

'Does that happen a lot? People just suddenly disappearing?'

'Not a great deal, but it does happen now and again, obviously.'

'Why obviously?'

'Well, because Julio disappeared. Therefore it happens, obviously.'

Tom looked around. They were in an enclosed area of about twenty metres square. The ground was mostly bare earth; scattered about were bits of discarded machinery, rusting. In one corner there was a wooden hut with one side missing; the roof was mostly intact affording some shade from the hot midday sun. A few rickety wooden chairs and a large wooden bench were piled up next to the fence.

'Help me move that bench out of the sun, would you,' said Odette. Together they hauled it into the shade. Odette picked up a grey blanket from a corner of the hut and spread it out over the bench.

'There. Now we can sit comfortably.'

'That blanket's a bit musty,' said Tom.

'Sorry it's not freshly laundered, Your Highness.'

'Very funny.'

'Well don't be so fussy, Tom, it'll do. Sit down, make yourself comfortable.'

Tom sat down; it was more comfortable than it looked.

'Have you brought many blokes here?'

'That's none of your business, Cousin Tom,' Odette blushed. 'Anyway, I told you the girls and I come here for peace and quiet. It's very restful.'

'Yes, I can see that, although Chloe and Anna don't strike me as being the sort of girls who are keen on peace and quiet.'

'No, they're not very keen, they do take some persuading sometimes. They don't like to stay long either.'

She reached down and opened her satchel. 'I've got a bit of food in here, not much really, just some fruit and a bit of bread and olives. Would you like some?' She sat beside him.

'That's great, thanks.'

She took out three battered aluminium containers and a flask of water. 'Help yourself, Tom.'

Tom tucked in eagerly to the fresh figs and apricots and washed it all down with gulps of water.

'You just happened to have all this food with you in case you felt peckish, did you?'

'I was supposed to have a picnic with my father but he didn't show up. Sometimes he can't get away at lunchtime.'

Tom stretched and leaned back on the bench. Odette edged closer, she smelt of sweat. 'Comfortable?' she said.

'Very, thanks.' Tom looked steadily at her; Odette lowered her gaze.

'Take your head scarf off will you, so I can see you properly.'

'OK,' she slowly pulled it off her head and shook out her short mousy brown hair.

'That's better,' he said.

She giggled.

'So, Tom, what brings you to Spain?'

'I might ask you the same question.'

'We've been here a while. We lost everything we had in the tsunami. My grandparents drowned.'

'I'm sorry.' Tom touched her damp fingers; she opened her hand and he held it. 'That must have been terrible for you.'

Odette blinked back tears. 'Yes it was. There was just me and my parents left. We had only the clothes we were wearing. No possessions, no house, nothing left at all.'

'How awful.'

She sniffed. 'There were hundreds of us in the same boat. Lost everything. Then the Muslims turned up with food and water. They put us all in coaches. My mother was in a state of shock, she just kept saying "Thank God, thank God", all the time. She got ill on the coach but the Muslims looked after her, gave her medicine and stuff.'

'So they brought you to Madrid?'

'Yes. I remember that first day, queuing up with so many people. We had to stand for hours and hours. The officials were walking up and down the queue and handing out cloakroom-type tickets from a bundle. One of them asked "Are you a family?" then tore off a strip and gave the three of us each a ticket with the same number 475. I'll never forget that number.' She frowned and looked pensive. 'Do you want to hear about this?'

'Yes.'

'When we reached the front of the queue there was a man wearing a filthy long robe, sitting behind a battered desk. He wrote down our names. He asked Dad if we had any baggage. When Dad said we lost everything he didn't even look up. He said "That's irrelevant" very coldly. It made my skin shiver.' Odette trembled. 'Then Dad was separated from us and me and Mum went into this prefabricated cubicle. It was so dark going in out of the blazing sun, like a cave. When my eyes adjusted I could see row and row of black fabric arranged on shelves. It was hot and there was this horrid smell of sweat. There were three women in there all in black – old fierce impatient women. I remember their faces were like white ovals, it was quite spooky. They told me to undress, there and then. I remember this old woman saying, "Hygiene is important, filth brings disease." I kept saying no but my Mum was so ill after standing for so long, she pleaded with me, so I undressed. Then this old woman got really near me. I remember it so well, I could see the wrinkles on her crabby

91

old face and I felt her breath smelling of spice on my cheek.'

Odette grimaced.

'Poor you, go on.'

'Then she said, "Hands over your head," and forced me into this long black gown and pulled my hair out from underneath the collar. Then I saw another woman with her hands in a tube of black fabric. I said, "What's that for?" and she said, "That's for your head." I said I wasn't going to wear that and she said, "It's modest to cover your hair and head otherwise men will leer at you and think you're a slut."'

'You didn't resist?'

'No, Mum could hardly stand up by that stage; I just had to go along with it. I remember the fabric being pulled tight over my forehead and ears and under my neck. Then they put a scarf over it and pinned it under my chin.' She gestured with her hands. 'Once I was dressed like them the old woman smiled. "Now you look respectable," she said. Then they opened the back door and told us to queue for food. Almost all of the women that side were in black, except some grey-haired women.'

'They didn't make your Mum dress like that?'

'No, they said she was too ill to get changed.' She frowned at him. 'You look shocked Cousin Tom.'

'So that's how you came to wear black.'

'Every day since then. I'm used to it now, but I don't think Chloe or Anna will ever get used to it.' She stared at him intently for a moment. 'You know, you probably won't believe this, Cousin Tom, but sometimes I don't mind wearing it, in fact I like it.'

'Like it? Yes, I am surprised. Why is that?'

'Well I was fifteen when the tsunami came and there were these things going in Alicante, well all over Spain, all

92

over Europe in fact, that I didn't like. Things young people were all doing and that I would be expected to do.'

Tom shrugged, 'What things, I haven't heard of anything.'

'I was a bit young but I knew I'd have to get involved sooner or later.'

'Sounds intriguing.'

'Well, I had this older cousin you see, Rosalyn, and she told me all about it. They went to clubs where they all watched pornography together and then they used to go into booths and have threesomes and foursomes and you always had to be with at least one stranger.'

'Doing what, like playing short tennis or something?'

Odette sniggered.

'Oh, don't look so vacantly at me, Cousin Tom.'

'Well, what was it they were doing, and what's pornography? Is that the right word? I haven't heard of it before.'

Odette's eyes widened.

'My God, you are so old fashioned! It's everywhere, everyone does it, it's just normal.'

'What's normal?'

'Where have you been living?'

'In the mountains, a remote community.' He bristled.

'You really don't know, do you?'

'Anyway, you said you didn't want to do it.'

'No I didn't, I was scared. I want to sleep with just one person, maybe the whole of my life. I don't want to sleep with two or three people at a time.'

'Is that what a threesome is?'

'Yes.'

'Hmm, what a strange idea. You've just got one prick and one fanny, why would you need to be with more than one person?'

'That's what I think.' Odette took a deep breath. 'We're both really unusual, Cousin Tom. My friends couldn't bear to commit, terrible word, shackled to one person. That's why they'd like to sleep around, but of course they can't now. They hate all these Muslim restrictions, they think they have the right to have fun and pleasure wherever with whomever they want.' She looked coy suddenly. 'Look, I don't know why I'm telling you all these things, I haven't told anyone before. My mum doesn't want to talk about it and Chloe and Anna; well I couldn't tell them, they'd just think I was uncool.'

She looked at him inquisitively. 'Look, what sort of civil partnership contract do your parents have? A one, a two or a three?'

'You've lost me now.'

'What, you've never heard of it?'

'Never.'

She shook her head. 'Amazing. It's the modern version of the outdated marriage contact. A level one is a five year commitment, a level two ten years and a level three twenty years.'

Tom frowned and shook his head. 'So, when your contract is up you just move on to someone else.'

'Yes, people get bored with each other you see.'

'So people must have several mums and dads.'

'Yes, most of my friends have two or three mums and dads, one after another and sometimes at the same time.'

'At the same time?'

'Yes, triple civil partnerships.'

'That sounds so complicated. My parents have been married for twenty-two years. They committed for life.'

'My God, you do come from the dark ages? Is everyone married in your community?'

'Married or single, yes.'

'Marriage now just means a great big wedding party, no more than that. My parents have a level 3 contract, that means they've got two years to go before they can happily go their own ways, but they say they're going to extend their contract if they can because they want to stay together.'

'A bit like old-fashioned marriage then.'

'That's what I want. So you see, when they put me in black, part of me thought, I won't have to do all those threesomes and foursomes that I'm scared of although I know I'm like, well old-fashioned and different and things, but then you're old-fashioned and different, aren't you?'

'As I said, I've never heard of these things before.' Tom tilted his head. 'So there are certain good things about being a Muslim.'

'Yes, all the Muslims are married in the old fashioned way. They think they're saving us from the terrible corrupt western civilisation, and well, maybe they're right.'

'So are you Muslims now?'

'My mother has taken Shahadah but I haven't, not yet; they don't force you to but many people have. We all attended the University of Simple Living. They taught us about Islam and I think it's a good way to live. Twenty years ago people were scared of Islam, there were suicide bombers everywhere and extremists, but it's very different now. You know I really understand how angry they were about their Palestinian brothers being turned out of their houses when the Israelis moved in. They felt they had no voice. Nobody cares about that now of course with so much of Israel under water. Anna and Chloe resent it but go along with it because they have to; they're not as happy about it as I am.'

'They seem a bit empty-headed. Not like you, you're much easier to talk to.'

Odette smiled coyly.

'What about you, Tom. Where are you from with all your old fashioned ways? You said something about mountains?'

'My friend Erin and I live in Switzerland.'

Odette looked crestfallen.

'Is she your girlfriend?'

Tom laughed. 'God no, she's old enough to be my mother. She's sort of a family friend, I've known her all my life.'

'Do you have a girlfriend back home?'

'No, I'm footloose and fancy-free.' He grinned. 'Are you allowed to have a boyfriend?'

'Not really, some do and get away with it.'

'Would you like to?'

'I would but nobody ever looks at me.' Her reply was so quiet Tom could only just hear her.

'Hey,' he said softly, squeezed her hand and looked into her eyes, 'do you believe in love at first sight?'

'I don't know. I suppose so. Do you?'

'I didn't before, but I do now.'

Odette lowered her eyes and blushed. Tom lifted Odette's damp hand to his lips and kissed her fingers; he felt them tremble.

'Lie down,' he said.

'Tom, I don't think... ' she began.

'Shh,' he said, putting the tip of his finger on her lips. 'Trust me.'

Odette stretched out on her back on the blanket, Tom lay next to her, his elbow resting on the bench, his hand supporting his cheek.

'Comfy?'

'Very.'

Their faces were now only a few inches apart. Tom looked searchingly into her eyes, leaned forward and kissed her. He could taste apricots and smell her pungent body odour. He opened his mouth and felt the soft tongue against his, making circles. I could probably go all the way, he thought, but better not risk it, first things first.

'Oh, Tom.'

For some minutes they clung to one another in silence then sat up close, facing each other.

'So how long are you going to be in Madrid for? Have you and Erin come here for good?'

'We don't plan to stay long.'

Odette looked sad. 'Why have you come to Madrid?'

'We've come to fetch an associate of ours. He's supposed to go back with us. We need him in Switzerland.'

'Where are you staying?'

'We're staying with some friends who live here; they have a house in the city, they're putting us up.'

'Not refugees like us then.'

'No, these are local people.'

'So when are you and your friend going to leave?' Odette plucked nervously at the blanket.

'That depends.'

'On what?'

'We have to get together with him first.'

'So he's not at the house you're staying at then? Where is he?'

'Actually he's in the detention centre, poor Carlos. We don't know how long he's going to be held there.'

'Have you asked the authorities?'

'No, we can't.'

'Why not?'

'I can't say.'

'Tom, please. You can trust me. I... care for you. I won't ever do anything to hurt you. You can tell me.'

Tom sighed. 'Well, you remember I said we live in Switzerland?'

'Yes.'

'We live in a community. The New Islamists... they're trying to find where we are and destroy us. We daren't do anything to draw attention to ourselves.'

'Who are they?'

'A branch of the Muslims who see us as their enemies.'

'So what are you going to do? Just wait until he's released? That could take weeks, or even months, depending on what they've locked him up for. What is it he's supposed to have done, anyway?'

'We're not sure. Something about undermining the authorities in Madrid we think.' Tom squeezed Odette's hand. 'Can I really trust you?'

'Of course.'

'We're not going to wait. We're going to get him out, somehow.'

'How on earth are you going to do that?'

'That's the tricky bit. We haven't managed to work it out yet,' said Tom looking down.

'I'll help you,' said Odette and squeezed his hand.

'I don't think that's a good idea. You mustn't get mixed up in this. It's dangerous.'

'No, Tom, honestly I want to help. I can be very useful to you.'

'How?'

'My father works in the detention centre. He's one of the officers. I can get inside information for you, the layout, the routines of the guards, all sorts of things.'

'Wow, that's amazing Odette.' Tom frowned. 'But I'm not sure... I don't want to put you in danger. I'm not going to see you get hurt or in trouble.'

'Please, Tom, let me help. I'd do anything for you.'

'Well,' he said doubtfully. 'Maybe... '

'Please, Tom, please.'

'All right, I'll ask Erin and the others.'

Odette kissed him on the cheek.

'You won't regret it, Tom, I promise.'

Odette's face shone with excitement. For a moment he felt a pang of guilt but quickly suppressing it, he leaned over and kissed her again.

'Tom, Tom, I'm so glad we've met.'

'We'd better go,' he said.

Odette put on her headscarf; they collected up the remains of their picnic and walked hand in hand to the gate. Tom swung it open and stepped through. Odette turned and looked back at the hut, the patch of waste ground.

'What is it?'

'I was just having another look at it. Now it's our special place.'

'Yes it is.' The place of my triumph, he thought but did not say.

*

Erin walked briskly, looking straight ahead; Tom lengthened his stride to keep pace. They reached the deserted wide open road. Tom heard the distant sound of a car. A piece of litter turned cartwheels as it was tossed along by the wind.

'So you're in love?'

'We might be.'

'Pigs might fly.' Abruptly Erin stopped as if rooted to the ground. Tom halted, he felt her hot piercing look.

'Erin, I thought you'd be pleased, she's on our side. She wants to help.'

'I'm very glad that she's agreed to help. God knows we need her. But I didn't expect you to dupe her, to lead her on in this way. It's wrong, Tom, you know that.'

'Are you saying I shouldn't have done it?'

'Yes! No – I mean - oh, I don't know.' Erin glared at him. 'I didn't want it to be like this. I should never have agreed to your approaching her in this way.'

'Why did you?'

'Well, if you must know, I didn't think you could do it.' Erin stopped and hugged herself, arms crossed against her chest.

'Well, thanks, Erin.' Tom looked away.

'You have done better than I expected with Odette, I just don't like the way it was done. You're feeling pretty pleased with yourself, aren't you?'

'Well... '

'You see, that's what's wrong – you misled her, fooled her, and now you're happy about it. You're patting yourself on the back, aren't you?'

'Well, I am a bit chuffed that it worked.'

'I hope you can live with yourself afterwards, knowing what you've done to that poor girl. I wouldn't have done it.'

'Oh no? So you'd rather let Carlos rot in there would you, to save your precious conscience? What would you do? How far would you go to get him out? Lie? Cheat? Steal? Kill?'

'Don't be silly, Tom. We must not do just *anything*. There are limits.'

'And what are your limits, Erin? Where do you draw the line? We all have to take personal responsibility for our actions, that's one thing at least I've learnt being in An Lac all these years. What about you?'

Erin turned to face Tom. She was breathing heavily.

'Well?' Tom said.

'What would Annando do if he were here?'

Tom smirked. 'Annando would stand there like the Buddha with love for all mankind pouring from every pore of his being and everyone would fall to their knees at his feet.'

'Don't be facetious, Tom.' Erin hiked away with her shoulders thrown back.

'You don't know what you'd do, do you? You don't know how far you'd go!' Tom shouted after her. 'You don't like it, do you, when you're challenged.'

CHAPTER 10

Odette's heart thudded as she climbed the last of the steps. She pushed open the front door and tiptoed through the cavernous entrance into the atrium. The walls were whitewashed and bare of any decoration. Two ceiling fans stirred the air desultorily, to little effect. Straight in front of her was a window. Through it she could see into a small office lit by a single light bulb hanging from the centre of the ceiling. To her left and right long sparse corridors stretched into the distance. Silently she removed her canvas shoes and tucked them into her belt. The stone floor felt uncomfortably cold on her bare feet. She flinched at the sudden sound of a loud snore. Creeping forward, she peered around the doorway into the little office. A guard was there, slumped in his chair. His head was cocked to one side, his mouth gaping open. On the desk there was an open leather-bound diary. As quietly as possible Odette stepped in and swivelled the diary round so she could see the entries. Nerves stretched almost to breaking point, she turned the pages, her fingers trembling. She stopped: there it was. An entry from two weeks ago, referring to a Carlos Zevez. According to the diary, Carlos was now in Bay 27. She hoped it was on the ground floor. She crept out of the office and looked at her watch. She estimated that she probably had about fifteen minutes before she would have to leave, successful or not.

Odette returned to the atrium. Should she take the left corridor? Or the right? She bit her lip, and looked first to the left, then to the right, then to the left again. Come on, get on with it, she said to herself. She scurried down the left-hand corridor as silently and swiftly as a mouse. She could hear shouting coming from somewhere, although she couldn't make out any of the words. Each of the bays along the corridor had a metal plate nailed to the wall beside it. The plates were numbered but seemingly in random order: 15, 20, 11, 12. There were smaller corridors leading off the main one but none had labelled bays, they just led to dead ends with rubbish piled up in the corners smothered in flies that buzzed lazily. She recoiled at the foul smell and could taste it at the back of her throat. Desperately Odette ran back to the atrium. To her relief the guard was still snoring. She took the other corridor passing Bay 9, then Bay 13. Next was Bay 25, then Bay 27. At last, she muttered breathlessly. She felt sweat trickle down her back, her robe wet and clammy against her skin. Then her heart sank: the bay contained four unmarked doors. Oh no, she thought. How on earth am I going to find which room Carlos is in?

She pressed her ear hard against the first door. A man was speaking: his voice sounded tense.

'You're crazy,' he said. There was a hollow cheerless laugh.

'Shut it,' said a second voice gruffly. 'This place is enough of a hellhole without having to share a cell with a shit like you. Another word out of you and I'll ram your teeth so far down your throat you'll have to shove your toothbrush up your arse to clean them.'

Odette quickly stepped back. Gingerly she pressed her ear to the second door. She could hear a soft rustling then the sound of someone urinating into a bucket. Wonderful, she thought. That's a big help. At the third door, there was a strong acrid smell as she pressed her ear to the cold metal.

'We didn't recycle because it was so much cheaper to send the garbage to developing countries and continue to extract more minerals, in spite of the social and ecological costs. We exploited these pitiable people and the rich, skilful in manipulating the system, just kept on getting richer.' Odette could hear the voice clearly, even through the metal of the door.

'The global corporations were the worst, weren't they?' said a second voice with a heavy Spanish accent.

'Yes, many of them had wealth greater than the GDP of a small country. Within them grey company men gave up their personal integrity and became automatons chanting the company mantra of "profit, profit, profit."'

Maybe this one is Carlos, thought Odette. There was a shout from further down the corridor and she shrank against the wall. After a few moments of silence she once again put her ear against the door. The men had lowered their voices and she strained to hear.

'You feel passionate about this.'

'I do. I blame the subversive advertising that seeped into people's subconscious. Either by actively participating in this or passively allowing it we are all involved in this destruction.'

'Even without knowing?'

'People think they have freedom but as Buddha found, even a palace can be a prison if it stops us from realising our full potential and knowing who we really are.'

'You're a visionary, Carlos.'

'I can't do much locked in here.'

Odette nearly squealed with excitement. She'd done it! Tom was going to be so proud of her. So proud that maybe he would... Blushing, she thrust that thought aside. Swiftly she ran back to the entrance. She couldn't hear the guard anymore! Odette peered round the door of the little office. To her relief the guard was still fast asleep, but now slumped forward with his head resting on the diary. Odette slipped her shoes back on, ran down the front steps and away, triumphant.

CHAPTER 11

The desert, Turkey

'How long is this bus journey?' said Ajit.

Ajit looked so small and frail in the shade of the palm tree, Stefano hoped the bus would come soon.

'Two hours from here into the desert, then we will need to ride camels for the rest of the journey.'

'I see, thank you.'

Ajit's kurta pyjama fluttered around his legs while gusts of wind created by ugly thundering juggernauts whipped by. Stefano peered at the timetable fixed to a rusty post. Its edges were brown and curved from the heat and the print had faded to grey. He squinted to have a better look.

'The bus should be here soon.'

'I see.' Ajit shut his eyes as a blast of wind blew dust into his face.

Heat haze shimmered above the grey tarmac in the blazing sun. Soon a rickety vehicle appeared and came to a stop with a screech. The motor clicked like a clock counting the bus' last seconds and the whole structure vibrated. Black smoke billowed from its exhaust. Stefano coughed as the tiny particles travelled down his nostrils; he felt his throat burn. The bus must have been red once, now only fragments of colour clung like parasites to the rusty metal frame. As they clambered aboard weary peasants with weather-beaten faces looked at them uninterestedly. Stefano took a window seat and Ajit sat beside him. There was an odour of chicken and dung. With a thundering vibration the bus roared away. They passed through the outskirts of a village with a roadside sign 'Beypazari' where colourful market stalls were laid out with fruit, vegetables and textiles and ceramics. Through the bus' dirty windows Stefano saw women in black chadors browse while men rolled worry beads between their fingers and played backgammon around coffee tables. A smell of strong scented coffee wafted through a small window and into the stifling bus. They passed by a refugee camp with rows of orderly white canvas tents. A few dirty children played football in the shade of a clump of palm trees. The driver accelerated and the bus pushed out to the open desert road. Endless rolling sand dunes disappeared into the misty horizon. The ruins of a few derelict breeze-block houses stood in the sand. A few sturdy cacti, battered into strange angles, clung to wind-worn rock formations. The bus pushed relentlessly on. The sun reached its pinnacle and began to dip. They passed white sun-bleached bones at the side of the road. Nearby two vultures flapped their wings and squawked. In the distance a lone Bedouin on a heavily laden camel flicked his stick unremittingly on the animal's neck. Hearing a thunderous roar from behind like an elephant's bellow Stefano turned around. A peasant in the row behind had fallen asleep and snored with his mouth opening and closing like a fish gasping in air. After another hour crossing pitiless open desert the bus pulled in at a roadside shack where a group of Bedouin with dark wrinkled faces squatted on their haunches in the sand. A trellis table was laid out with a heap of water melons. A line of camels was tethered to a metal rail.

'This is our stop,' said Stefano.

Ajit nodded. Stefano noticed Ajit's bloodshot eyes and grey complexion.

The driver cut the motor, unmasking the animated chatter outside. They climbed down into the baking heat. A lone Bedouin stood apart from the rest in a sleek white robe and black head wrap; there was a poise and authority about him as he held the ropes attached to three camels. This must be the man, thought Stefano.

'I am looking for a man called Malik,' said Stefano.

'Where are you heading?' said the Bedouin. In the man's voice Stefano could detect the hint of a refined English accent.

'We are Imam Jalal Kowi's guests. This is Ajit and I am his travelling companion, Stefano.'

The man's expression was inscrutable.

'Guests especially brought by Allah are always welcome. Jalal Kowi is my master. I am Malik, his humble servant.' He lightly touched his own heart and forehead in greeting.

A sudden breeze of hot air swept down from a nearby dune. Fine grains tossed in the air and into their faces. With one hand Malik adeptly swept his black head wrap over his face; only his eyes, like two restless black buttons, were visible. Ajit had shut his eyes and stood still and silent until the torrent passed.

The melons were slit into pieces and their blood-red juice dripped into the sand; the peasants sucked on them noisily. Saliva rushed into Stefano's mouth. He could faintly smell the melon's sweet juices and was filled with insatiable craving, but the Arabs eyed him suspiciously and didn't offer him any. With enormous will he stifled his desire. The three camels roared as Malik pulled vigorously on the thick ropes; one after another he brought them to their knees. Their heavily laden saddles were hung all over with tassels, white shells and blue beads.

'We each ride a camel,' said Malik.

Ajit tentatively approached one.

'Shall I help you?' asked Stefano.

'No, I don't need help,' said Ajit and pulled himself up.

They climbed on. As Stefano's camel raised its back legs he was flung forward and held on tight to two round wooden protrusions like doorknobs which were positioned front and back. The seat was made of carpet, now hard, compacted by the weight of riders. The camels were on their feet. Stefano looked down; the ubiquitous sand seemed dauntingly far away. They set off across the sand dunes. Looking back the tarmac road was only a hazy grey line in the distance, the bus a shimmering carcass of metal. The camels plodded at a steady pace. There was a heavy stillness, the only sounds the steady flicking and crunching of sand as the beasts' feet skimmed the golden depths. Soon Stefano got his balance, shifting his weight forwards and backwards as the camel rocked back and forth in a slow repetitive movement. At last the seat felt rigid and safe.

'Water hole another two hours,' shouted Malik. 'You should cover your heads from the sun.' He rode alongside and passed them both black and white checked shemaghs. 'Here.' They wrapped them round their heads. 'No, you have done it wrong,' he said. 'Like this.' He took off his own black shemagh, folded it in half into a triangle, put it on his head and adeptly twisted the two ends into place. Ajit and Stefano watched and followed his instructions. 'It is not right,' he said when they had finished, 'but takes time to learn.' He whipped his camel which broke into a trot and took his place at the front.

For what seemed like an eternity Stefano rode on aware of only sand, torrid heat and the crunching of the camels' feet. Every now and then he looked over at Ajit, riding alongside, sitting motionless and upright, his eyes shut.

As the sun set, the horizon turned a misty vaporous grey and Stefano felt a deep chill seeping into his skin. He squinted as a hazy mirage of green appeared on the horizon. He blinked again and again and thought for a moment he might be going mad. He poured some tepid water from his tin canteen into his parched sandpaper mouth, savouring every last coppery drop and swishing it around his gums and tongue. Malik pointed ahead to a clump of palm trees. 'Water hole,' he said.

As they drew closer, smudges of green were transformed into a circle of robust palm trees arranged round a pond flat like a mirror. Up close, lizards scuttled into tumbleweeds leaving the swirling impressions of their bodies as trails in the sand.

Malik's camel roared as he whipped it to its knees and down. The camels all down, they dismounted and the beasts slurped noisily at the water hole. Deftly, Malik unwrapped three small black nylon tents from the saddle pouches, erected them and put blankets inside. Vigorously, Malik pulled up a metal bucket from a well of crude bricks and decanted the water into three aluminium cups.

'Here, drink,' he said bluntly.

As Stefano poured the water down his throat it felt cool and fresh, like nectar.

They sat in a small circle. Malik put a leather bag fixed firmly with a piece of string on the sand, dexterously unlaced it and laid the contents bare. There was a smell of barbecued flesh. Grey strips of meat lay scattered inside. Small birds that had been bathing in the pool hopped nearby, watching.

'Here, eat.'

'But we're veg... ' Stefano tried to complete his sentence but Ajit put up his hand.

'When you are in Greenland the choice is between caribou and seal. Vegetarianism is not a realistic option,' he said and picked up a strip of meat. Stefano looked down again into the bag. Ajit has a point: better than starving, he thought. Although his stomach was tight with hunger, he recoiled; he hadn't eaten a piece of meat for some twenty years. Gingerly he picked up a piece between his finger and thumb and held it up. It stood upright by itself, stiff, bony and glutinous; there was gristle amongst the burnt flesh. It slipped slightly between his fingers as bloody grease oozed out. Malik bit noisily into his strip like a wild animal, tearing the flesh away with his incisors. He eyed Stefano strangely. Ajit was chewing slowly and steadily, with his eyes half closed. Hunger overwhelmed him. OK, Stefano said to himself, took a deep breath and bit heavily into the dead flesh. It was tough and stringy and tasted salty; pieces of gristle floated around in his mouth, he nearly retched. After a short battle between hunger and revulsion he ate three more strips until the leather bag showed only the smeared remnant of dead flesh. Birds jumped in and pecked at the spoils. Malik burped loudly and rubbed his stomach.

'We need to cook desert rat well to avoid stomach pains,' he said nonchalantly.

Stefano felt suddenly sick, saliva flowing into his mouth as if he were about to gag or vomit. After some moments the sensation subsided and his stomach felt strangely full.

'You have an unusual accent, have you always lived in the desert?' asked Stefano.

'I spent two years at a prep school in Tunbridge Wells when I was a boy, picked up some English,' said Malik. 'Oxford English they tell me.' He looked evasive, suddenly. 'Jalal Kowi is very respectful of Annando and his movement. He is a reasonable man.'

'Annando feels the same about Jalal Kowi.'

'It is a long way for you to come. It is Allah's will.'

Stefano looked over at Ajit who sat huddled in a ball, shivering.

'He's getting cold,' said Stefano.

'When the night comes the cold comes. Now we must get into the tents,' said Malik.

Stefano pulled up the zip of his tent and settled into the blackness. He could hear the wind whistle and the nylon fabric flap back and forth like the soft wings of a bird, but in the darkness of his mind's eye this bird was an eagle, predatory and menacing. A cold breeze slid around his face. He buried himself in the thin and ineffective blankets; they smelt of sweat, barbecued meat and smoke. Outside a camel's shrill murmur grew louder and became a deep gruff sigh. The freezing cold seeped from the hard packed sand through the flimsy mat and into his soft flesh. Gritty sand was locked under his fingernails. He was aware of his vulnerability; beyond the thin veil of the tent was the vast unforgiving desert. There is nowhere that's safe, he remembered Annando saying. It echoed round and round in his head. He'd always felt safe at An Lac, working the land and in the dairy. His days were quiet and predictable. An Lac seemed to him like an oasis of peace, harmony and community, a kind of paradise; that's what had attracted him in the first place. But as time passed he knew he was only fooling himself, clinging to an illusion. An Lac could only hide for so long. One by one people of the inner core had been sent on missions, out from their sanctuary into the chaotic, anarchistic abyss where extremism, immorality, corruption, power, influence and manipulation were the rules of the game and where you needed to be smarter and better informed to survive. Ironic really, that the one place where he could have an easy life had become a dangerous place to be and here he was sent on this precarious mission. He longed for the warmth, comfort and safety of his own bed, of An Lac. He heard a slow steady snore. Ajit, stoic, wise, resourceful and patient. Ajit, a man of few words and his words were full of piercing truths. Annando had chosen wisely. The wind gusted and Stefano could hear sand whipping against the tent, quick and shrill. He shivered. What if Malik were going to double-cross them? There was something shifty in his eyes. He might, he was Arab after all. He could abandon them here in the desert, he and Ajit. Without a guide they would both dry out like prunes in the midday sun and endure a prolonged and cruel death. He visualised them in his mind's eye. Their mouths and tongues dry and parched, their lips cracked and bleeding with pain, they'd cry out like deranged madmen, 'water, water.' Their eyes raw, blood red, they would fall to the ground and sand would seep into their ears, eyes, noses, every open crevice of their bodies. Hard and uncompromising grains would bind and settle like cement, their clothes stiff with dirt and sweat. They would shrivel up and take their last breaths. The camel outside groaned. He heard sand shift as it moved its enormous weight. A shiver went through his body and he rubbed his cold feet under the blanket. In the darkness he felt for his rucksack, loosened the cord, plunged his hand inside, felt for the smooth roundness of a boiled sweet, unwrapped the cellophane and pushed it through his lips. A strawberry flavour filled his mouth and he sucked on the hard sphere like a baby. Exhaustion swept through his body. His eyes closed heavily and he fell asleep.

*

He woke to the sound of rustling and camels moving. He could see someone's shadow outside the tent.

'Now we must get up.' He could hear Malik's voice, commanding and close.

Stefano unzipped his tent, bleary eyed. Ajit stood before him, alert and fresh, in his kurta pyjama and black and white shamagh, perfectly in position. He passed Stefano a mug of hot liquid; he smelt coffee and Ajit's sweat. Steam rose from the cup.

'Three hours to Jalal Kowi's camp,' said Malik.

After three hours' travel across dry rolling sand dunes Stefano saw through the heat haze a misty blink of colour on the horizon. As they rode steadily towards it the outlines of the blurry shapes sharpened into focus. A village of canvas tents packed together in a tight circle emerged out of the wilderness. As their convoy entered the village, Bedouin, clustering around a central well, looked in their direction. An imposing tent with walls made from colourful drapes dominated. At its entrance was a canopy supported by carved wooden stilts. A dirty boy ran up, took the rope of Malik's camel and led them into a space where camels, tethered to posts, lazed on the ground with their jaws grinding. The Bedouin round the well eyed them suspiciously. As he dismounted Stefano could feel his legs stiff and sore; he saw Ajit stretch.

'Come,' said Malik.

Inside one of the smaller tents it was surprisingly cool. The walls were made of canvas with black and white horizontal stripes, the roof of black densely woven fabric. On the sand was a patchwork of overlapping colourful Arabian rugs; scatter cushions in deep purples and reds lay around. An old man with a bent back shuffled in and gestured for them to sit. Balanced precariously in his hand was a shiny brass tray; on it was a ceramic pot and three tiny cups. They pulled up cushions, Ajit sat comfortably with his legs crossed. The old man squatted and put the tray on the carpet. As he poured the hot brown liquid into the cups steam rose and there was a strong smell of coffee. Gesturing, he urged them to drink. Ajit sipped cautiously.

'You must drink, it is a symbol of hospitality,' said Malik sharply. He stood nearby watching, his arms crossed.

Stefano downed the thick bitter coffee in one mouthful. A residue like brown silt lay in the bottom of his cup. He tilted the cup. The residue stayed in position like glue. Malik waved his hand impatiently at the man who quickly rearranged the items on the tray and was gone. Stefano shivered; he felt vulnerable suddenly in this alien, unpredictable place with strange rules of custom and honour, where an Arab could appear to love you one moment and knife you the next. The silence was pierced by a sudden bang of drums, clash of cymbals and the pounding of rhythmic music. Women sang in high, shrill voices. He noticed Ajit look up and turn his head towards the direction of the sound.

'Sufis,' said Malik decisively.

'Sufis here?' said Stefano.

'Jalal Kowi's wife is a Sufi,' said Malik.

Stefano listened, absorbed, while the music built to a crescendo and there was clapping and ecstatic shouting, a slow quiet tapering off into silence. After a few moments they could hear the subdued murmur of people talking. There was a sudden jingle of soft bells and a woman swept in and stood before them. Her long dark hair cascaded around her face and over the shoulders of her white fitted dress. Her black eyes shone, she panted slightly and her skin glowed. She looked from one to another then held Stefano's gaze steadily. As if gripped by an impulse she suddenly swirled on the spot and the bells on her anklet tinkled. Her enormous skirt ballooned; underneath he saw her slim legs in tight white trousers. Facing them, she came to a complete stop; the fabric of her dress cascaded back and forth, and was still. She grinned with happiness and looked intently at them. Looking up Stefano saw a smile creep over Malik's face. She walked a few steps towards them and held out her hand to Ajit. They stood up. Close up Stefano could see that she was not young, but she had the vigour and intensity of youthfulness and she had a natural and radiant beauty.

'My name is Sofia, Jalal Kowi's wife. You must be Ajit, he is expecting you.' Ajit nodded, his face serene. She turned to Stefano. 'But who are you?' Her voice sounded melodious and soft, like the music of a cool mountain stream.

He took a deep breath. 'My name is Stefano, I am Ajit's travelling companion. I am honoured to meet you.'

'Guests are always welcome, especially guests brought by Allah. Come,' she said and gestured with her arm. As she led them outside her dress rustled on the sand and the bells on her anklet tinkled. They could hear the slow beat of a drum. 'I will take you to meet my husband, but first you might like to see our dancing; it is very special.'

She led them into a larger tent crammed with people standing with their backs to the canvas walls, looking towards the empty space in the centre. Silence fell on the crowd as two women and four men dressed in tall red felt caps and white garments swept in. After a few prayers, the music began, ponderously, and so did the dancers stomping slowly to the rhythm of the music. As the music quickened, faster went their feet and round they went in a circular procession, twirling slowly then whirling on the spot with their arms held high and their heads tilted backwards, smiling ecstatically. Their enormous swirling skirts were like great rotating disks; the spectators clapped and chanted. There was a hot steamy atmosphere and a smell of frankincense and sweat. At one side of the tent was a trio of musicians, men dressed in long brown robes. The fiddler gyrated vigorously as his bow sped up and down the strings, his face contorted with concentration; he was flanked by a drummer and a man playing the flute. Behind them were flat circular discs of metal suspended by a shining red cord from a metal framework. Intermittently the drummer beat the discs with a stick and they wobbled back and forth sending a crash and vibration through the tent. Sofia's face glowed and she clapped her hands.

'Whirling dervishes,' said Sofia.

'Quite a sight. The dance is very beautiful,' said Stefano, raising his voice above the music.

'It is a meditation,' said Ajit.

'Yes,' Sofia said and looked over at Ajit. She whispered in Stefano's ear, 'He has a serene face, as if he were full of divine love.' She looked back at the dancers.

Stefano leaned towards Sofia, so as not to shout. 'How is it a meditation?'

'It is a worship ceremony. By listening to music, focusing on Allah and spinning in repetitive circles you abandon your ego and personal desires. The aim is to reach the source of all perfection, the kemal.'

'And why the dress?'

'The camel hair hat represents the tombstone of the ego, the white skirt represents the ego's shroud.'

They watched for a few moments.

'The dancer's expressions are blissful,' said Stefano.

Sofia nodded in agreement.

'So, how long have you been a Sufi?' he asked.

'It is my tradition. My father was a Sufi and his father before him. We are from the Mevleviyah order. But I am the first woman in my family to perform the Sama.'

Sofia clapped her hands in rhythm with the music. Women spectators wailed as if in frenzy, their mouths open and their tongues moving rapidly from left to right.

'Are you blissful when you are whirling?'

'Many people think the dancers are in ecstasy, in a trance, but it is not a trance. For me it is a moment of great clarity, when I am completely absorbed in the dance. Some dancers hear the subtle sounds of the spiritual realm and attain higher knowledge. I have not experienced anything like that and I have no desire to.'

'You express yourself in English very well.'

'I like to read a lot, and to dance.'

Malik stood nearby, motionless and watchful.

'Well, now I will take you to my husband.' She led them into the imposing tent with the colourful drapes.

*

As they passed under the canopy Stefano examined the stilts close up; Arabic script was intricately carved into the wood. The entrance was covered by a curtain of heavy red fabric.

Sofia pushed it aside and they went in. It was suddenly cool and there was a smell of incense and fresh fruit. As his eyes adjusted to the semi-darkness Stefano looked around: it was lit by candles in exotically patterned brass lanterns suspended on metal chains from the ceiling. There was a muted noise like water from a babbling brook. A line of tall poles supported the middle of the tent, whilst the front, back and sides were supported by shorter ones; the floor was covered in thick Arabian rugs in reds, oranges and yellows. Colourful tapestries hung from the walls. There were several shining brass tables piled high with pieces of melon and coconut. Stefano held his breath; the sensory experience was almost intoxicating. At the back of the tent was a platform with a seat on it, set like a throne. It was surrounded by sumptuous cushions.

Stefano swallowed. 'Is this Jalal Kowi's seat?'

'It is.'

With his eyes now fully adjusted Stefano could see in the half-darkness two Arabs sat lazily in a corner smoking a glass and bronze hookah. Each had a separate mouthpiece decorated with colourful stones. Their inhalations sounded like sucking: a hazy smoke billowed around them.

'Do you like it in here?' asked Sofia.

'I do, it feels like a cave,' said Stefano, 'it's heady and exotic.'

'I chose all the interiors myself,' said Sofia. 'Jalal would prefer simplicity, he is a modest man, but because I designed it, he tolerates it. I think he likes it, but he won't admit it.'

In the muted light he saw the silhouette of a man entering from the back of the tent. 'Peace be upon you, you have honoured us at this blessed hour,' said a strong rich voice. He walked towards them; he was tall, dressed in a crisp white robe and checked hattah. He had a long grey beard. 'I see you have met my wife, Sofia. Come here my dear.' Sofia went to him and held his hand, she looked up at him tenderly. 'Isn't she the most beautiful creature? I would keep her locked up if I could, but she craves freedom. Isn't there a saying, "Set a bird free and if it comes back it always was yours, and if it doesn't, it never was."?'

Ajit took a step forward. 'It is an honour to meet you Jalal Kowi,' he said. 'I am Ajit, and this is my companion Stefano.'

'Ajit, the pleasure is all mine,' said Jalal Kowi. Lightly, he touched his own heart, then his forehead, he fixed his eyes on Ajit, taking him in.

Jalal Kowi took his seat on the 'throne' and gestured for them to sit around him; Stefano sank down into sumptuously soft cushions. Jalal Kowi raised his head and snapped his fingers. From behind a drape decorated in peacock feathers, a young servant appeared.

'It is getting late and our guests must be tired and hungry. Bring food, and plenty of it,' he said, and with a flick of his hand waved the servant away.

CHAPTER 12

Madrid, Spain

Raphael opened his eyes and sat forward, 'So what time does it start?'

'About 9 o'clock,' said Aziz.

Erin squeezed the last of the water from the rag and put it in the sink. 'What time does what start?'

Raphael rubbed his chin. 'Aziz has a cousin who's said to be taking part in some kind of weird beauty contest at Paradiso.'

'The clandestine shopping centre place I've heard so much about?'

'Yes, we're thinking of going along; maybe talk her out of it. From what we've heard it's not your normal affair. Definitely not something you'd want any girl mixed up in.'

'I'll come as well,' said Erin.

Aziz frowned. 'I'm not sure that's wise; it might get very rough. It's not for the easily shocked. You know, you live in the spiritual community in Switzerland.'

Erin glared at him. 'Don't patronise me, I don't shock easily; besides I could be useful helping to persuade her to leave with us.'

*

The square of artificial light from the open doors lit up the darkness at the back of Paradiso: they crept up and peered around the side of the doors. It was packed and there was shouting and animated banter. The crowd faced a stage where a man in a smart suit and bow tie sashayed up and down talking into a megaphone. Above him hung a sign in orange neon lights, 'Bob the God seeks wife.'

'Blimey.' Erin took a deep breath.

'Sure you want to go in?' said Aziz, studying her.

'Yes, we definitely need to get that poor girl out.'

Erin, Raphael and Aziz sneaked in unnoticed and stood in the shadow at the back. Inside the atmosphere was humid and steamy; there was a smell of beer and cigarettes. They listened.

'... that God of recent history was worshipped by the quirky, old-fashioned and feeble-minded. That's dead. We're modern and we have our own living God.' The crowd applauded and shrieked. 'After the stimulation of the first five heart-stopping shows we now come to the spectacular final of our competition,' said the host. 'In the front we have our five finalists picked by ace footballer of the beautiful game, Bob the God. Tonight, one of them will be selected to be Bob the God's w-w-w-wife!' There were more shrieks. Intrigued, Erin stepped on a chair to get a better look. Five girls in bikinis, three white, one black and one Asian, were lined up on the stage. A white girl with beehive hair had a sign of the cross on the fabric across each breast and on her bikini crotch; the black girl had pink polka dots and lacy bows on her bikini and the Asian had a g-string studded with diamante - on each breast was a Star of David. 'These five sexy girls Zoe, Clara, Mona, Yolanda and Minx (as he said their names each stepped forwards and raised her arms) have made it to the final and here's their chance to show Bob the God just how sexy they are!' There were raucous cheers and wolf whistles. A group of men near Erin went 'rawwww' and gulped down their beer. 'He likes big boobs, but if you're not DD girls you'll have to find other ways of making him happy. Make sure you've got your own condoms and sex toys, girls, and I'll let you into a secret, he likes S and M.' Erin gulped, Oh God, this is worse than I imagined, she thought. The crowd roared, someone shouted 'Yes!' and another 'Get them off!' 'It's a simple test, girls, in a few minutes, behind that screen, each of you will have five minutes, yes, just five minutes to fuck Bob the God and he'll choose the girl he likes the best to be his wife.' The crowd screamed, driven into a frenzy.

A man nearby cupped his hands around his mouth and shouted, 'Get rid of the screen!'

The host continued, 'Tonight we're launching a new sex potion all the way from Germany that Bob the God is promoting. There's 20% off tonight and it'll be on sale at the end of the show so you can try it yourselves ladies and gentlemen. I bet there isn't a girl in the room who wouldn't want to bend over with her pants down and be fucked by Bob the God.' The host bent over, flicked his jacket over his back and pulled his pants down displaying his white buttocks. The crowd roared. He pulled his pants back up. 'Each of our runners-up will get a certificate signed by Bob the God saying that he's fucked her. You lucky girls, that's a passport to celebrity status that will impress your friends!' The girls on stage screamed and jumped up and down like puppets. 'The winners will be announced in reverse order, third, second, then the lucky bride! The winner is guaranteed the wedding of the decade with no expense spared. Five Rolls Royces, up to ten bridesmaids of your choice, eight different designer wedding dresses to wear one after another on your big day and a reception fit for the status of Bob the God! There may be poverty and global warming outside but when you're God's wife nothing but the best will do. This is the stuff of dreams.' The crowd cheered and the girls gyrated provocatively.

Erin leaned towards Aziz, 'Is your cousin one of the five?'

'No, thank God, she must not have made it to the final.'

Erin gulped and climbed down from the chair. 'I've seen enough.'

'I'm sorry you came,' said Aziz, 'I thought it might be something like this.'

'Let's go.'

Just at that moment two burly bouncers slammed the doors shut. Erin felt the blood drain from her face and she came out in a cold sweat.

'I'll find another way out; stay here,' said Aziz.

'So all I need to do now is introduce Bob the God.' In a pitch of excitement the host shouted, 'Here he is!'

There was a drum roll. With dramatic effect a curtain was pulled back and a man stood there dressed in a gold shirt and tight shimmering white trousers emphasising his crotch. Above his head a neon light in the shape of a halo gave off a spectral glow. It was supported on a thin rod held in place by a white bandana wrapped around his forehead. He held his arms open, looked at the crowd below, flashed his Day-Glo teeth and swaggered across the stage. The crowd went down on one knee, wide- eyed, hands together in prayer as they gawped at Bob the God. For a few moments he stood there.

'You may stand,' said Bob the God when the drum roll finished, and drew his arms upwards with a dramatic flourish.

The crowd stood up. Some people started to cry, others were breathless.

'There's another way out,' said Aziz. 'It's near the stage so we'll have to push our way through.'

'Let's get out,' said Erin, sweating.

'Stay near me.'

Aziz, Erin and Raphael set off. They passed a woman reeking of strong perfume and a man whose breath was potent with alcohol. The host interviewed Bob the God as they pushed between breathless hot bodies. Erin felt the front of her shirt being pulled down and a hand squeezing her breast.

'Nice tits, let's see a bit more of them.' The man's face was red and beaded with sweat, his eyes feverish.

'Get off!' Erin pushed him away. Raphael punched him and he fell back into the crowd: once down people gathered round. They let him lie there with the detachment of children looking at an insect; then a man kicked him in the ribs.

Raphael put his arm around Erin as they pressed on, 'Are you OK?'

'Yes.'

Zoe got up on the stage and gyrated provocatively to the sound of 'Love to love you baby,' before she and Bob the God disappeared behind the screen on which was written in bold glittery text, 'God's Choice.' Disco music played and people danced until she re-emerged, topless, and suggestively licked her sex toy to the delight of the audience. Clara gyrated then disappeared behind the screen. For a few moments Beethoven's fifth symphony pierced the disco music. They reached the doors which were open a crack. A bouncer stood in the space, grinning, with his hand down his trousers, absorbed in watching the show.

'Better wait for a moment,' said Aziz.

There was standing room only. Erin felt her heart thump. She stood with her back against a wall, said her mantra and closed her eyes. The cool concrete on her back and hands brought relief. Someone stood on her foot, sending a rill of pain through her leg; someone elbowed her as they went past; she put all her concentration on her mantra. There was a drum roll. Warily she opened her eyes.

'And now we'll ask all five girls to come up on stage so we can announce the winners.'

The girls tottered in their stilettos into the centre of the stage. There was a sharp scream, one of the girls fell; her face was contorted in agony and she had her hands around her ankle, one shoe off. Two bouncers pulled her off the stage and the doors were flung open.

A male voice shouted, 'Out!'

The girl howled, 'But I might have won.'

'Bob the God doesn't want damaged goods; he's the best and he wants to be seen only with the best. You're injured so you're out of the running. Now get out of here,' he said savagely.

He handled the girl roughly by the arm and flung her out into the darkness while the crowd laughed and looked at her with contempt. There was a moment of chaos while the host talked with the bouncer and returned to the stage.

'Minx is now out of the competition, but we still have four sexy girls left... ' he said.

'And in third place is... ' There were a few moments of silence then a drum roll.

In the commotion Aziz, Erin and Raphael pushed their way outside. The cool fresh air hit them like a slap. Minx lay crumpled on the ground, bawling, with her hand on her ankle. Out of the darkness two rough men appeared and grabbed Minx, yanking her to her feet. One pushed his hand between her legs.

'You're hurting me!' screamed Minx, struggling to get free.

'Leave her alone!' shouted Erin. She felt her body quiver feverishly.

The door slammed shut, and all was quiet; they could see only dully, by the light of the moon.

Raphael grabbed one man's shirt collar from behind and wrestled him to the ground. Aziz kicked the other man in the groin. He doubled up in pain and fell to his knees.

Minx cowered into a ball and whimpered as the four men faced each other. Erin stood between them, close to Minx, her fists raised.

'You have two choices, Minx,' said Erin. 'You can go with these men, or with us. If you come with us I give you my word, we won't hurt you.'

'I want a wedding with Bob the God,' squealed Minx, 'I don't want to go with any of you.'

'That's all over now, like the host said, that's the stuff of dreams. This is reality. These are your stark choices, us or them.'

'Leave me alone.'

'If I do that these men will take you away, and I don't think they want to marry you.'

'I haven't got my certificate; they promised me a certificate, celebrity status. They promised.' Her voice was thin and frail. Aziz's opponent leapt to his feet and with a roar charged at Aziz, his arms outstretched, ready to grab and crush him. Aziz sidestepped and simultaneously kicked the man in the knee. The man fell heavily, clutching his leg and groaning. The other man got up and lurched at Raphael. They wrestled. Raphael punched him in the chin; the man staggered fell back and lay still.

'I think they've lost interest in you now,' said Erin, 'let's get out of here.'

With an arm over Raphael's shoulder and the other over Aziz's Minx tottered along on one leg with her damaged foot dangling above the ground. Erin walked in front, glancing around now and then to make sure they were still following. The streets were deserted; the pavements glistened wet in the moonlight. All Erin could hear was the click-clack of Minx's stiletto on the hard pavement and the occasional quiet sob. The journey seemed interminable. Eventually they arrived at the safe house. Erin unlocked the door and stood aside as the trio went in. Raphael and Aziz placed Minx gently on Erin's bed and left the room. Minx shivered and whimpered, her face smeared with rivulets of black mascara and red lipstick. Erin covered her with a blanket and exposed her damaged foot. Close up she smelt of a mixture of beer, aftershave and male sweat. Erin picked up a clean towel from the bathroom, split it open with a razor and tore it into strips.

'I'm going to bandage you up.'

She sat on the edge of the bed and put her hands around the thin white ankle. Minx's flesh was smooth and cold. Erin picked up a false eyelash from the blanket and placed it carefully on the bedside table. She wrapped the towel round and round Minx's ankle, glancing at her from time to time and feeling Minx's angry and suspicious glare.

'It's best to keep the ankle elevated if you can,' said Erin putting a pillow underneath Minx's ankle, 'it will help reduce the swelling.'

'What do you want from me?'

'Nothing. You were hurt and in danger. We were able to help.'

'You're a liar. You're New Islamists in disguise, aren't you?'

'No, we're not,' said Erin, quietly.

'You want me for a slave.'

Erin stood up, went over to the work surface near the window and put on the kettle.

'I'm making a hot drink. Would you like one? It's good to drink.'

'I've no money,' said Minx.

'No charge.'

Minx gave a short barking laugh.

'Nothing is free, you phoney.' Her face screwed up with bitterness. 'You're going to make me your slave, aren't you?' Her eyes narrowed.

'You're free to go whenever you like.'

'You're just pretending.'

Minx rubbed her eyes and the eyelash dropped off. She felt her eyelid for the other.

'I've lost an eyelash,' Minx said, and gasped in distress searching frantically for it on the blanket.

'I've found it, it's here.' Erin walked across, showed it to her, and went back to the kettle.

'Thanks.' Minx's voice softened and she was thoughtful for a moment. 'They've got my shoe, my sex toy and my clothes; I don't know when I'll get them back. My toy was blue; do you know where I can get another blue one?'

Erin took a deep breath.

'I don't know anything about that sort of toy. I've never used one.'

'Never used one? You're weird; everybody needs one.'

The kettle whistled. Erin brought two hot chocolates over and sat on the side of Minx's bed. While Minx sipped her drink, Erin's mind wandered. She remembered Richard, the loving look in his eye and the soft touch of his hand. After he died she lay in bed and her body shook for days. She had thought the emptiness would never leave her. Then she met Annando and experienced his unconditional love. Inexplicably, since then she'd barely had a horny thought or feeling, her sexuality had simply died, either that or gone into long term hibernation.

'They said I'd get a certificate and become a celebrity, but they just kicked me out.' Minx's eyes welled with tears; she looked at Erin steadily, searchingly. 'Which celebrities do you like?'

'I don't know of any celebrities.'

'You are weird,' said Minx.

Erin rummaged in the wardrobe and pulled out a couple of items.

'Here, you can borrow this shirt and these trousers.'

'Can I use your make up and curlers?'

'I can't help you with that,' said Erin.

There was a knock on the door.

'Come in,' said Erin.

127

Raphael stood in the doorway.

'Do you want to meditate with us?'

'Yes,' said Erin.

Erin looked at Minx. 'I'll be back in half an hour.'

Minx stared intently at her as she walked away.

*

After the gong, they opened their eyes and talked softly, sitting cross-legged in the subdued light around the candle. The door crashed open and Minx stood in the doorway dressed in Erin's clothes. Her bandaged ankle dangled and the false eyelashes were back in place.

'You people,' said Minx, wide-eyed as if she had suddenly had a revelation, 'are you the people they call the mystics, followers of Annando?'

The four looked at each other, then back at Minx.

'We are,' said Erin.

Minx's jaw dropped open and she gawped at them. 'My Uncle Rick talks about you people all the time. He says the New Islamists are out to get you. Are they really after you?'

'Yes they are, unfortunately, they're trying to find our ashram,' said Erin.

'What's an ashram?'

'It's a sort of community.'

'My Uncle Rick says he can give you something to help you.'

'Really, do you know what it is?'

'Naah, summat you can make he says, but I don't know what.'

*

As she approached the café Las Margaritas Erin saw Minx through the dirty window. She was sitting next to a burly man in his forties with a ruddy face. The flimsy red door of the café screeched as she opened it and flapped back on its hinges. There was a musty smell and the walls were stained grey. A few customers sat at tightly packed table and chair units that were fixed to the laminated floor. Minx and the man were in the corner, deep in conversation. When they saw her approach Minx whispered something in his ear.

'Hi, I'm Rick, Minx's uncle,' his voice was gruff and he held Erin's gaze steadily.

Erin squeezed herself into the chair opposite.

'You people were good to Minx when she was in trouble.'

'We were glad to help,' said Erin.

A bored waitress in a stained overall came over. 'What can I get you?'

'Just a coffee,' said Erin.

'Will do.' She walked away.

'Minx told me what those people running the competition did. When she fell they threw her out in her bikini. They didn't even give her her clothes or sex toy. They slammed the door on her, treated her like a piece of dirt.' His tone of voice was indignant and he grimaced.

'That's right,' said Minx.

'She'd paid the entrance fee and worked hard getting through the rounds of the competition. If she hadn't slipped she might have won the wedding. They didn't even give her a certificate, and she's fucked Bob the God. She came away with nothing.'

Erin took a deep breath and said, 'Maybe it was unwise to take part.'

Rick held her gaze steadily, his expression full of sincerity. For some reason she trusted this rough weather-beaten man.

Minx's face screwed up and her eyes were alive with hate and revenge.

The waitress dumped the chipped cup onto the table; some coffee sloshed on to the saucer. She sauntered away.

Minx elbowed Rick, 'Tell her.'

'I've had enough of those people at Paradiso, they're rotten to the core and the New Islamists are dragging people in. I don't trust them either. Everything's going to the dogs. Minx says you're the mystics, followers of Annando. I've heard about you people and have been trying to track you down, but you're an elusive lot.'

'We need to be, to protect ourselves.'

'You're the only hope. If not for you we'll either be tearing each other apart or be forced to pray all day. I want to help you.'

'Go on,' said Erin. 'Minx said you can give us something. Is that true?'

'If you have access to additive manufacturing equipment, then I do.'

'What's addictive manufacturing equipment?' asked Minx.

'Additive,' said Erin. 'It's another name for 3D printing, where you manufacture a solid object by building it up in layers. Yes, we have additive manufacturing. We make the plastic raw materials ourselves from special crops.'

'Good, I can give you the blueprint for a hand weapon like a pistol. It's called a Hanzza device. It might be useful if your hideout is found.'

'We're not strong on violence,' said Erin.

'There are two settings: one kills them and one knocks them out.'

'How does it work?'

'There's a powerful capacitor in the handle that holds a hefty amount of electric charge. You have to use induction coupling from an electricity supply to fill it up. When you pull the trigger that charge is used to generate a beam of electrical energy. Direct the beam at someone's head and it causes the brain waves to resonate, building up more and more energy. Depending on the setting you either kill them or they become unconscious. If you don't kill them they'll come round, probably with a splitting headache but no lasting damage.'

'Sounds just the thing,' said Erin, 'I'm very grateful.'

'One good turn deserves another,' said Rick. 'Here are the details.' Rick passed Erin a fingernail sized piece of crystal.

'Encrypted, I presume?' asked Erin. 'What's the password?'

'Bob the God,' said Rick.

'Great,' said Erin. 'I'll have no difficulty remembering that.'

CHAPTER 13

Tom heard the muezzin calling the faithful to the mosque for Friday midday prayers.

'Now!' came Raphael's muffled voice from behind. Tom felt his heart pound. He lifted his chador and felt for the first step, trying to keep his balance. He felt strangely vulnerable, with only a limited view through his eye slits. At the top of the stairs he pushed the heavy metal door and stepped inside. He quickly crossed the atrium, with Raphael close behind. They entered the small office. Behind the desk sat a lone guard, making pencilled notes in a file. The man looked up.

'This is no place for women. Where are your husbands?'

Tom held out a piece of paper in his gloved hand. The guard took it and read it quickly. He gasped and his eyes widened. Slowly he stood up, his hands by his side. Tom saw a pistol in a holster at the man's hip.

As the guard moved away from the desk, the telephone rang shrilly: Tom stood transfixed, staring at the desk as the sound filled the room. Swiftly the guard drew his pistol. Raphael burst forward, launched himself at the guard, pinioning his arms and dragging him down to the floor.

'Quick Tom, help me take him,' he hissed. His hand shaking, Tom took out his cosh and struck the guard hard behind the ear. As they stood up the ringing stopped. 'Good man,' said Raphael. 'Now let's get his uniform and hide him somewhere. You grab his legs and I'll take his arms.' They manhandled the unconscious man into a small storeroom, undressed him, trussed him up, gagged him and locked him in.

They took off the robes and stuffed them into their rucksacks. Raphael put on the uniform, checked the pistol carefully and replaced it in the holster. Taking the guard's place at the desk he settled down to read the files, his rucksack concealed at his feet.

Tom went into the adjacent office. Feverishly his eyes scanned a board on the wall studded with metal hooks holding sets of keys; all seemed to be duplicates. He took a set and went further into the building down the right hand corridor; he heard a man cough and a toilet being flushed. Tom made straight for bay 27. He approached the third door, hoping that Carlos hadn't been moved since Odette had found the correct room. The door was made of solid grey metal studded with steel rivets. Tom put his ear to it; he could hear the faint murmuring of subdued voices. His hand trembled as he tried key after key in the lock, his sweaty fingers slippery on the metal. With only two keys left to try the lock clicked releasing the bolt. As he pushed the door aside it creaked on its hinges. He went in. There was a putrid smell of body odour and urine.

A man stepped forward. He was an imposing figure, taller than Tom, with a full, grey-flecked beard.

'I'm Pablo; we got the message and have been expecting you. We're eager to leave this place, but one of us is badly hurt.'

Tom peered into the darkness. 'How many of you are there?'

'Just three.'

As his eyes adjusted to the light Tom saw a row of mattresses stretching down one side of the room. At the far end was a recumbent figure, with another crouched over him: Carlos. As Tom drew near he could see the man lying with his eyes closed but his breathing was laboured, his face grey and lined.

'Who is he? What happened to him?'

'His name is Bertrand,' said Pablo. 'He was like this when they brought him back after the latest bout of questioning a short while ago.'

133

Now Tom saw that all three men had cuts and bruises on their arms and faces. His heart sank.

'Can he walk?' he asked.

'I don't know,' said Carlos. He shook Bertrand, trying to rouse him.

Bertrand moaned softly, and opened his eyes.

'Bertrand,' said Carlos, 'we have a chance to escape.'

'Escape?'

'Yes, can you stand?'

'I think so; it was mainly my arms they worked on. Nearly pulled them out of their sockets, but I should be able to walk. Help me up.'

As gently as they could, Carlos and Pablo sat Bertrand up; as he clutched their shoulders they lifted him bodily until he was able to stand.

'How's that?' asked Carlos.

'I've felt better, but I'll manage.'

'Good,' said Carlos.

Carlos clasped Tom's right hand with both of his. 'Tom, well done for getting in here and releasing us. Quite frankly, I didn't think you had it in you. Ralph will be very proud of you.'

'I've had a lot of help. And we're not out yet.'

'Quite right, I was getting ahead of myself.'

'Tom, I would also like to say thank you on behalf of Bertrand and I,' said Pablo. 'You are a very brave young man.'

'We don't have much time,' said Tom, 'we need to get out before the midday prayers finish and the guards come back to work.'

Carlos opened the door and peered into the corridor. 'All clear.' He crept out beckoning them to follow.

Raphael stood up sharply as they reached the reception desk. Within moments he and Tom were back in disguise.

'Are you coming with us to the safe house?' asked Tom.

'No,' said Pablo. 'Bertrand and I will leave Madrid immediately. I have relatives in a village not far away. We will take shelter with them, at least for the time being.'

'Well, good luck to you both,' said Carlos, 'who knows, we may meet again someday.'

'Inshallah,' said Bertrand with a chuckle as he and Pablo waved goodbye.

'Our turn now,' said Carlos, heading for the steps. Erin and Odette standing watch on the pavement gave no sign of recognition as they passed. Carlos strode briskly along with his two 'wives' following a few steps behind. They walked past the billboard 'Bienvenidos al distrito de negocios de Madrid' across the dual carriageway and into the town.

They came to a small café with a scattering of tables and chairs set out on the pavement. Carlos led the way indoors and they all sat at a table in a secluded corner. Erin started to say something but Carlos held up his hand, cutting her off.

'Who is this?' he demanded, indicating Odette. 'What is she doing here?'

'This is Odette,' said Erin. 'She gave us vital inside information, and she has been standing watch with me outside; she was going to send any returning guard on a spurious errand for her father.'

'Her father?'

'Yes, my father,' said Odette. 'He's an officer at the prison.'

Carlos' face went pale. After a moment he leant forward, flashing his most charming smile.

'Odette, I wonder if you would be good enough to step aside for a few minutes, please. I need to discuss something private with Erin.'

Odette's eyes narrowed, and she gave a curt nod.

As she got up, Tom stood as well.

'I'll come with you.'

Odette gave him a quick smile, evidently pleased. She reached for his hand, then remembered his disguise and stopped. Odette headed for the women's toilets, and stopped outside as though waiting for someone.

'You were great today,' said Tom. 'That inside information was just what we needed, and standing watch, too.'

'I'm glad. I did it for you.' She took a breath. 'Your friend, the one who got out, he doesn't trust me, does he?'

'He has to be careful. He doesn't know you.'

'It's OK, when he gets used to me, I'm sure it will be better.'

Tom went very still. There was a long pause.

'You bastard!' she hissed. 'That's it, isn't it? I helped you, now you have no further use for me, I'm being dumped. You little shit! I thought you cared for me. What a fool I've been.'

Tom hid under the chador, unable to meet her gaze or look into her face twisted with fury. He said nothing.

'I've a good mind to tell my father all about you.'

Now Tom looked at her, stricken.

'Oh, don't worry I'll not betray your little secrets. I have more self-respect than that. But you can't go round doing this, you know. Using people, then discarding them like used tissues.'

Abruptly Odette turned and hurried out of the café into the bright sunshine. Tom watched until she was out of sight, then went back to join Carlos and the others.

CHAPTER 14

An Lac ashram, Switzerland

How did Stefano manage to stay so cheerful doing this grubby tedious task, never complaining, never wanting or needing to be thanked thought Ralph as he stood in front of the white stone fireplace. No one noticed because it was always done, as if by some invisible benevolent goblin. Ralph stooped down, pulled out the tray from underneath the grate and tipped the ash into a hessian sack. A thin cloud of grey ash wafted around him. Inhaling, it smelt of burnt wood. They'll notice my effort though; I just haven't got the patience or stamina for this. Stefano must have done it as a true meditation in which case he's a better man than I.

He lifted the heavy iron grate away from the hearth and on to the wooden floorboards, took a brush from the tool stand, swept from the back of the hearth to the front and shovelled the debris into the sack. He laid some newspaper on to the flagstones, lifted the circular brush from the tool stand and put one foot inside the hearth. Without bending his legs, he bowed under the lintel, straightened up and stepped fully inside. The air felt cool. He looked up into blackness and felt up high with his right hand for the hook Stefano had told him was there. With his fingers he felt the cool smooth curve of the metal and the sharpness of the point. He took the torch from his pocket, turned it on and suspended it from its looped cord onto the hook. It sent a diffuse light downward and illuminated the vast greyness of the chimney. Up high he could see a small patch of daylight.

He heard quick footsteps and Isabella's soft melodious voice, 'Ralph!' Suddenly he felt her gentle hand on his leg. A second later she was inside the hearth, standing close facing him. He felt himself itch.

'Isabella, you'll get filthy in here. I'm about to clean the chimney.'

'This was one of Stefano's jobs, wasn't it, before he went away?'

'Well, he's not here, so someone has to do it.'

'You do everything now, Ralph. Everyone's gone. Tom, Erin, Stefano and Ajit. They won't be coming back will they? There's only you and me now to run An Lac.' Her voice held a trace of fear.

'Hardly. You, me and one hundred other people.'

As his eyes adjusted to the darkness he could see her cheeks were flushed and she held his gaze with a passion he didn't recognise. The top button of her long white gown was undone and his eyes were drawn to her cleavage. The braided cord was drawn tightly around her waist emphasising its narrowness and the feminine swell of her hips.

'And the tsunami will come and we'll all be washed away like my brother and drowned.'

As she spoke he could feel her warm breath on his cheek and smelled the scent of clean cotton and jasmine.

'We're on the top of a mountain, we won't be washed away.'

'The rains will fail and dry up and the crops will die and we'll all starve to death,' she said breathlessly.

'There's plenty of water.' He heard the rasp in his voice, he swallowed hard. 'Take a walk, some fresh air, you'll feel better.'

'I need to talk to you, Ralph,' she whispered urgently.

'Not here, not now... your white dress.'

He felt a wave of apprehension.

'Ralph, I'm having these strange feelings,' she gazed at him intently, 'feelings in my body I've never had before.' Her eyes flashed and with her lips parted she put her dainty hand gingerly on the collar of his shirt as if touching something completely unfamiliar, uncertain how it would feel. 'I have such strong desires.' With intense concentration she slowly moved her hand downwards, towards his waist. He froze, aware only of the sensation of her hand on his shirt, moving. She stopped at his belt and gently pushed her fingers between his trousers and shirt. She lifted her fingers out and smoothed her hand over the flies of his trousers. He looked into her cleavage, and her full white breasts, now heaving. There she stood, only inches away, raw, beautiful in the half-darkness and full of unexplored lust. Ralph was aware of the frightening intensity of Isabella's passions, he felt desire sizzle through him. He was a trapped rat, drowning in the gutter.

'Tom was sweet, but he's young and very fast. I need a mature experienced man like you Ralph. You know I've always loved you, like a brother until now, but now I want you.'

There was a soft rumble and a clump of soot fell from above. The torch began to sway wildly from left to right. Ralph put his right hand up, feeling for the cord. He felt the cold hook on his thumb and a sudden sharp pain. Instinctively, he pulled his hand down.

'Ralph, are you hurt?'

'I think I've pricked myself; it's nothing.'

As he steadied the torch with his left hand she grabbed his right hand and put it under the light.

'Your thumb is bleeding.' Her voice was soft, full of concern.

He put his left hand on her head to brush away some particles of soot and her hair was soft, too soft. Slowly she pulled his thumb into her mouth and sucked. He felt the softness and warmth of her lips and mouth. She gently pulled his thumb away and gazed up at him.

'You see, you are part of me now. Kiss me, Ralph.'

She moved her mouth close to his and looked up at him, her trusting eyes wide with anticipation.

'Isabella, I can't,' he said softly.

'Why, Ralph?'

He hesitated.

'Because we're both standing inside a chimney and because I'm married.'

'Why, Ralph?' she repeated as if she hadn't heard his reply and pressed herself against him. He felt the softness, warmth and ripeness of her.

'No, Isabella,' he said feebly, feeling his resolve weaken. Shit, he thought, I mustn't, this would be a bloody disaster. He felt an instinctive sexual quickening within him, an overpowering urgency which was more of nature than man. Get a grip, for God's sake, he said to himself. His face was burning hot and his heart palpitating wildly.

The gong sounded, the familiar, reassuring and deep friendly boom. Ralph came to his senses. He pulled away. 'Come,' he ducked under the lintel and pulled her through after him. In the light her cheeks were flushed, her chest heaving and her face full of anguished disappointment.

'You're not yourself, get some fresh air.' He quickly turned and walked to the door.

'Ralph,' he heard her call after him.

Briskly, he crossed the hall and went into the garden. He gulped in the fresh air, walking fast; a rush of relief swept through him. He felt the cool wind on his hot flesh and looked out at the wide expanse of sky. Just got out in time, thank God, he thought, but he still felt the desire pour through him. Cool down, cool down, he urged himself, but the desire kept flowing.

He flung open the front door. Jane was standing by the sink with her hands deep in the frothy washing up bowl; she turned and looked at him.

'What is it Ralph, you look frantic, what's happened?'

140

He stood for a moment and looked at her in her yellow rubber gloves and apron, almost a uniform now. The long plait cascaded down her back and her brown dress looked dowdy and utilitarian, but that did not cool the fire of desire that burnt in him.

'Are we alone?' he said bluntly.

'Yes, they're all at school.'

'Come on, let's go upstairs.'

Jane's eyes widened; submissively she peeled off her rubber gloves and stared at him with an expression which was a mixture of both puzzlement and pleasure.

'Ralph, at last.'

He took her hand and led her upstairs. In the bedroom there was a smell of dirty laundry, the curtains were closed and the duvet in a messy heap.

'Give me a minute,' he said.

He dashed into Tom's room and pulled out the top drawer of his cupboard. There, underneath Tom's Y-fronts, he found the packet of condoms he'd got for Tom months before. He pulled a sealed condom out and tore the blister. He went into the bedroom. Jane was in bed. In the half-darkness he kissed Isabella's soft lips and felt his hands on her dainty waist; he felt her soft flesh hot with desire.

*

He rolled onto his back. Jane twisted herself around him and lay her head on his shoulder. He felt her breath on his cheek.

'Ralph, there was such a passion in you today. You see, it's so easy to use a condom, then I don't have to get pregnant again. I'm so pleased you've seen things my way at last. It's not natural for us to live like brother and sister, keeping it all pent up.' Her voice was quiet and affectionate.

She made circles on his hairy chest with her finger. 'It's not right, we're married, and we need to express our love.'

Ralph looked up at the ceiling, his body stiff as if held in a vice.

'What is it? Don't punish yourself; you're only a man, an ordinary man. Talk to me, Ralph.'

Abruptly Ralph pushed her away. He sat on the edge of the bed with his head in his hands.

'Ralph, don't go cold on me, we should be tender with each other, especially now.'

'Don't talk,' said Ralph, roughly.

He hurried to the bathroom, removed the condom, cleaned himself, washed his hands and splashed water on his face. Looking up he caught sight of his reflection in the mirror. He'd often been told he was good looking. He examined himself critically. He saw his thick hair dishevelled, his face flushed and his brown eyes bloodshot. He rubbed his shaven skin and could hear the rasp of his bristles. Yes, maybe he was still good looking in a mature sort of way, but this was a picture of Dorian Gray; he felt only revulsion at his own image. The real Ralph was a weak inadequate man, full of lust, deceit and untamed emotions. He was suddenly nauseous. He felt the stomach acids seethe and climb up his oesophagus.

Jane knocked violently on the door calling 'Ralph, Ralph!'

He knelt down and clasped his hands on either side of the toilet bowl; putting his head over the toilet he vomited.

CHAPTER 15

The desert, Turkey

'I have only one wife: she would be offended if I took another, and indeed I need no other. Until Khadija died Mohammed had only one wife whom he loved dearly and who was entirely his equal. Sofia is my Khadija.'

'He is the ideal husband,' Sofia gazed up at him.

'You are Ajahn Annando's representative. It is my pleasure to welcome you, in peace. Please accept my hospitality.' Jalal Kowi gestured for them to sit and settled himself into the soft sumptuous cushions. Stefano took his place warily, aware of Ajit calm and serene on his left and Malik stiff on his right. 'Tell me how I can help you.'

'I am here because Annando holds you in high regard: he knows that you, like the prophet Mohammed, have a reputation for honesty, integrity and fairness. He told me I can speak openly to you,' said Ajit.

Jalal Kowi raised his chin, smiled and looked around at the assembled company.

'Speak then, and you shall be heard.'

'Annando is seeking your support to revive spirituality. His aim is nothing less than the transformation of the remaining populations, to establish a world full of spiritual communities. He wants to restore the religions: not restore the institutions that have been built up over the centuries and became morally bankrupt but to foster the shared experience of the inner reality that lies at the heart of all true religions.'

Two Ethiopian men with skin like polished ebony came into view. One carried a low brass table which he set down in the circle in front of Jalal Kowi, the second put a large platter of steaming food on to it. They rose, backed away, bowed and exited. The smell of rice and spices made Stefano salivate; he realised how hungry he was.

'Tell me, how does Annando view Muslims?' said Jalal Kowi.

'He is very respectful; he holds Islam to be one of the great religions of the world.'

'And you? You are a Hindu, are you not?'

'It is true that I was born a Hindu.'

'And now? What do you believe, as an adult?'

'Gandhi said that the sayings of Mohammed are a treasure of wisdom not only for Muslims but for all mankind. I think he was right.'

Jalal Kowi gave a muted laugh. 'Gandhi was a great man.' He sighed, and looked thoughtful. 'I too want to see more spirituality in the world.'

'Your reputation as an honourable man is well known.'

'I have always tried to live like the prophet Mohammed himself.' Jalal Kowi mused for a moment, and pulled distractedly on his long grey beard.

'You are the best of Muslims,' said Sofia sitting close to him. She looked at Jalal Kowi tenderly.

Jalal Kowi smiled benignly at her. Turning to the others, with a wave of his hand he indicated the platter of food. 'Please come, eat.' On the platter circles of flat bread were arranged around a brown mixture sprinkled with pine nuts sitting atop a huge mound of white rice. One of the Ethiopians brought in a plate filled with slices of blood-red water melon. Jalal Kowi picked up a piece of bread, scooped some mixture on to it and gulped it down in three bites. Stefano watched the others do the same; following their lead he scooped up the mixture and ate greedily. He struggled to identify the tastes, turmeric, certainly, and paprika; other tastes were unfamiliar. He gave up and let himself enjoy the food. The other Ethiopian gave a bowl of clean water and a starched white linen napkin to each diner.

Jalal Kowi dipped his fingers in his bowl and dried them on the napkin, the others followed suit; he sat back and frowned. 'The catastrophe of global warming was caused by the excesses of a secular, liberal and greedy society. That society stretched across the globe, too big to be controlled and destroyed itself. As a result we live with anarchy; now people behave as if they are beasts in a jungle.' His voice was flat and devoid of emotion, as though he were confirming the minutes of a business meeting. 'And Annando really believes that he can change that, to establish spirituality?'

'I agree it is extremely ambitious but he is determined to do it.'

'Brutality leads to lawlessness and vice versa. My Muslim brothers and I are trying to help people; we are putting order back into their lives, order and meaning. People need religion.'

'Indeed without religion there are no absolute moral values, only social conventions,' said Ajit.

Jalal Kowi chuckled. 'With anarchy, there are no social conventions, my friend. The advantage of Islam is that we have a clear moral code which is understood by all.'

'Other religions also have social and moral codes.'

'They have, or rather they did. These religions are fragmented and lack leadership. The secular society had penetrated all the other mainstream religions: only Islam is strong enough to withstand those pressures.' Jalal Kowi leaned forward and looked intently at Ajit. 'My friend, look at what happened in Western society: so many single mothers and boys without male rôle models running wild like feral children. Gay and threesome marriages against nature now commonplace and a lifestyle choice for many who live without guidance. Pornography everywhere, seeping into every aspect of peoples' lives corrupting their thoughts and their speech. No respect for women or family life, the obsession with beautifying one's body, the worship of youth and the frenzied pursuit of longevity.' He sat back. 'Ruthless capitalism is to blame, it fed people's greed, their crazed desperation to have more and more material things. As a result we have had all these climate changes, making millions into desperate refugees. Those that have survived the devastating pandemic, that is. We are helping them and educating them to live simply: so many things are in such short supply, there is no other feasible way to live.'

'I agree that living simply is the best way forward. However, is it right to force people to pray, and women to dress in black robes in order to eat? This is not charity alone, this is coercion, surely?' said Ajit. 'With all respect, would Mohammed have supported this?'

'There is no coercion: refugees have accepted Islam willingly, their hearts have been opened,' said Jalal Kowi, frowning.

Stefano saw Malik squirm on his cushion and stare at Ajit with narrowed eyes; he swallowed hard.

'When Mohammed set up the Constitution of Medina he established duties, rights and responsibilities, and the rule of law for a civilised state. It was very practical and one of the earliest known models of governance. It included Jews, Muslims, Christians and pagans. Mohammed accepted all these people as part of the same nation, the Ummah,' said Ajit.

Jalal Kowi stroked his beard. 'Yes, this is true. All the tribes and people of different religions signed it and were all subject to the same laws.' He leant over and picked up a piece of bread, dipped it in the mixture and chewed it slowly.

'In Mohammed's final sermon he said that the ultimate reality is all one and that all tribes and nations are equal before Allah. One man is superior to another only by way of piety and good deeds,' said Ajit.

146

'All this is true.'

'Later Muslim leaders disregarded this part of the message and marginalised themselves, defying the message of the prophet.'

'This is also true,' said Sofia, smiling at Ajit.

Ajit continued, 'For Mohammed there was no compulsion in religion. "You to your religion, me to mine" he said. Each one of us should make a free and willing choice. He preached equality and inclusion.'

'Your knowledge is impressive: you are obviously a learned man.' Jalal Kowi looked ponderously at Ajit.

Malik picked up a chunk of melon in one hand, his knife in the other. As the blade tilted towards the light of a glass lantern it flashed orange. He examined the knife for a moment then savagely cut through the pulp. 'Master, this Hindu infidel knows nothing.'

Jalal Kowi held up his hand. Malik grimaced, put the piece of melon in his mouth and chewed it fiercely. Red juice flowed down his chin; he wiped his chin on the sleeve of his gown.

'The Koran is a sacred book but, with due respect, sadly some passages are open to interpretation as is Sharia law,' said Ajit in a steady voice.

Jalal Kowi's eyes narrowed and he pulled forcefully at his beard. Stefano took a deep breath and looked at Ajit who sat serenely still.

'Indeed on the whole Islam is a tolerant religion,' said Jalal Kowi. 'We recognise the prophets of Judaism and Christianity but, and this is the important thing, these religions are now weak and offer no effective guidance. Desperate people need to be shown the way. When people come to Mohammed, peace be upon him, they will see the way and then they will be saved, physically and spiritually.' His voice was slow and confident as if the idea was a truth in itself and he had had the last word. He picked up a small piece of melon, carefully placed it in his mouth, and sat back again.

'So in your view, only some of humanity can be saved? A select band that live by your rules? I am a Hindu by birth – what are my chances of being saved?'

Jalal Kowi gave out a short barking laugh. Under his breath Malik muttered 'Infidel!' He grabbed his knife and adroitly stripped the skin off a piece of melon. Stefano felt Malik's indignation radiating like a force field and he began to sweat. He lifted his cushion from under himself and moved it along a few inches nearer to Ajit; Sofia leant towards Jalal Kowi.

'I know what Annando is teaching: he encourages people to go back to the roots of their own religion. He says that the origin of all religions is in the experience of the same universal truth. We should all meditate then we will be transformed. We are all spiritual beings and the truth is inside each of us,' said Jalal Kowi.

'I see you have grasped the essence of his teachings,' said Ajit.

Jalal Kowi coughed gently, his hand in front of his mouth. 'I have read his works. But he is naïve. Never in the history of humanity has there been complete agreement. There are different religions, different cultures, different rituals and practices. But there is only one way to salvation, by the five pillars of Islam.'

'So for you the path lies through following rules, not by revelation?' said Ajit.

'The only way to salvation is through Allah – and that means Islam, you ignorant fool,' hissed Malik through clenched teeth.

Jalal Kowi raised his hand in admonishment. 'Have a care, Malik. Let our guest speak.' He cleared his throat. 'These are trying times to be sure.' Stefano detected a note of irritation in Jalal Kowi's voice. 'Man must live by rules, otherwise he will be overwhelmed by his animal instincts.'

'Isn't there a danger in every religion, including Islam, that the rules and the rituals become more important than the spiritual revelation that can be found through contemplative prayer, meditation and even sacred dancing?' Ajit gestured toward Sofia. 'My own experience and observation has shown me that each one of us has the potential to be transformed and to behave differently, with honesty and discernment, because we understand deeply; we know it at a level even deeper than the intellect, and have touched the sacred.'

'That sounds familiar; Sofia tells me much the same.'

'Ajit is right. Like a dirty cloth that gets washed over and over again and becomes whiter and whiter, so Sufis when we are completely absorbed in the whirling we are more in contact with our true infinite selves. Whatever our religion it is the same for each one of us,' said Sofia.

'Yes, I agree. Mahatma Gandhi said religions are different roads converging at the same point. What does it matter if we take different roads, we are all seeking the same truth,' said Ajit.

'For Sufis and others exploring spirituality, people like yourselves perhaps: most are not like you,' said Jalal Kowi.

'But they all have the potential, whether they know it or not.'

'That's right, Jalal. Everyone does,' said Sofia.

'My dearest, it seems you are already one of Annando's disciples.'

Sofia leant over and put her hand on Jalal Kowi's.

'I will always be a Muslim and proud to be one, my love.'

Jalal Kowi studied her thoughtfully and rubbed her hand with his thumb.

'Hmm.' He turned towards Stefano. 'We have not heard from you. Do you agree with Annando, Ajit and Sofia? Where do you stand?'

Stefano felt his cheeks burn, he swallowed hard. 'I... I... er... he stammered, 'I agree with Ajit,' he said. Stefano shifted on his cushion.

'Ha! Of course you do.' Malik spat on the sandy floor, glaring at Stefano.

'Do you have an answer for Annando?' said Ajit. 'I am eager to return with good news, that you will join us and help with the spiritual resurgence.'

'Annando's impetus is to be welcomed. Humanity is desperately in need of a spiritual revival. I am happy to do whatever I can to help him. Furthering the spread of Islam can only be good.'

'As you know, Annando's aim is to revitalise all the religions, not just Islam.'

'Islam has the virtue of being the only religion not subject to moral decay, unlike the others.'

Ajit cleared his throat. 'Sadly that is not true. There are the corrupt imams such as Ali.' Jalal Kowi sat up straight and looked sharply at Ajit. 'He is an example of the opposite: his liking for strong drink is very well-known as is his use of prostitutes. This is the worst kind of hypocrisy is it not, to live one way and preach another? Imam Mahdi is almost as bad, as I am sure you are well aware.'

'Insolence!' Malik's eyes flashed as he glared again at Ajit. 'Master, give the word and I will throw these infidels out!'

'These are wicked slanders, against men of God. Rumours and slanders, with not a shred of truth.'

'You are mistaken. Many know of their wickedness.'

'How dare you speak to Jalal Kowi like this? This is an insult!' Malik brandished his dagger at Ajit.

'Put that knife away, Malik', said Jalal. 'Violence is not necessary. Ajit will apologise for his discourtesy.'

'I mean no disrespect,' said Ajit. 'But you must hear the truth. You are wrong to trust Ali and the others.'

Abruptly Jalal Kowi stood and rose to his full height.

'Enough! I will hear no more of this. They are my friends and allies. I stand with them. A slur upon them is a slur upon me. You are no longer welcome here. You must leave. Tell Annando of your failure here. Malik, you will escort these guests back across the desert, but treat them well.'

Jalal Kowi swept out of the rear of the tent.

'You will regret that you ever came here,' hissed Malik hurrying after Jalal Kowi.

'That was not good.' Sofia laid her hand on Ajit's arm.

'What do we do now?'

'You must do as he says. You must leave, quickly. I will help you to get ready. Come.'

Ajit followed her out of the tent with Stefano close behind. The blinding sun and dry heat stung Stefano's eyes and pricked his skin. Arabs stood around in quiet groups eyeing them suspiciously.

CHAPTER 16

Stefano woke with a start from his fitful sleep; he heard the sound of a tent being quietly unzipped, then a muffled cry. He thought he might be dreaming. As his eyes adjusted he detected the first rays of dawn sunlight; the black nylon walls of the tent had turned a murky charcoal grey. There were more muted noises outside and a smell; he sniffed the air. No, it can't be, he inhaled again. Oh God it is! His heart pumped and he trembled. A visual memory in all its colour and intensity played itself out like a movie in his mind. A goat's throat was being cut, the blood draining into the gutter and with it that metallic smell. Adrenalin coursed through him and with the speed of a scuttling lizard he flew out into the bright sun.

Ajit's tent was open; there was a trail of blood in the sand. Shaking, Stefano peered inside. Ajit lay in a pool of blood. He recoiled and for a moment everything went spinning before his eyes. He took a few backward steps, stumbled, panted and let out a wild cry. In front of him he saw the dark silhouette of a camel on its knees and Malik adjusting the ropes.

'Do not bother with him, he will be dead soon,' said Malik, levelly.

'Why? He did you no harm,' said Stefano, his voice reedy and thin.

'He was a politician with clever ideas. I need to protect Islam.'

'You are a murderer,' howled Stefano, stumbling again.

Malik gave him a cold penetrating glance. Stefano shuddered violently; he felt his muscles turn to jelly and fell to his knees. His face burned hot and his heart palpitated wildly. From somewhere he heard a groan.

'Oh God, Oh God! Ajit, Ajit!' He bolted upright and dived into Ajit's tent.

With a surge of courage he deftly pulled Ajit out and into the sun and cradled him in his arms. 'No, no!' Bright red blood seeped from the corner of Ajit's mouth, his face white, his skin cold and clammy. 'Don't leave me,' whispered Stefano. A chest wound bubbled blood; it made a sound like a soft hiss. The smell made him nauseous; as he breathed he tasted it in his mouth. He shuddered.

Ajit looked up at him wide eyed, his mouth moved, but he uttered only indistinct, broken sounds.

'What, what?' Stefano's breath came in short sharp bursts.

'It is the end for me,' Ajit mumbled.

'No, no, don't go!' Stefano's voice cracked and he felt his heart might burst.

'My time has come. You must carry on.' Ajit's voice was faint and feeble. 'Tell Annando... '

'Tell Annando what?'

Ajit gasped, 'My death was not in vain.'

Ajit coughed suddenly and with one great spurt blood gushed from his mouth. He wheezed for several seconds and was silent. Stefano felt blood seep, warm and sticky, through his trouser leg and on to his skin. Ajit's body softened and became flaccid.

Malik's camel roared as it stood up. Stefano saw through the blur in his eyes that the three camels were tied together. There was a terrifying bubble of comprehension. Malik was going!

'You're leaving us here, without a camel?'

'Yes.' Malik sat tall and straight, with his hands on the ropes.

Stefano rested Ajit's body on the sand and stood up.

'Then you have as good as killed me as well.'

'You are not important. It is written, there is no other God but Allah.'

'If your God is that small, petty, jealous and greedy, you can keep him. This is not an Islam the prophet Mohammed would recognise. This is barbarism, the anarchy you pretend to despise. You are no better than the worst of them,' he said in a hoarse, gasping voice.

'You are a weak, simple man and you rave like a lunatic. Sacrifices have to be made for the jihad. When Islam has taken over, then your people will understand.'

'Then God help planet earth under Muslim rule.'

'You blaspheme, infidel, now I return to my master.'

Malik whipped his camel and it turned, the camels roared and their feet flicked sand as the convoy moved off.

'Animal!' shouted Stefano.

Shaking, Stefano knelt back down and cradled Ajit's body in his arms. Turning his head to the sky he yelled, 'Where is the justice when good men die and bad men run free? Where is the justice?' He wailed so loud his throat became dry like sandpaper as he rocked Ajit steadily in his arms. He was aware only of the agony of that moment, not how long that moment was. As time passed the vigorous rocking became a slow mournful rhythm and his wailing a murmuring lament. The heat rose as the sun climbed in the sky. Gently, he placed his fingers over Ajit's eyelids and closed the vacant eyes. He was aware of his impotence in the face of his own inevitable impending death. He, Stefano, deserved to die. He had failed to protect his precious cargo. Ajit's body felt heavier and heavier; Stefano's muscles ached, as if in a vice. The bloody smell became strangely sweet, intoxicating, numbing; he breathed it in. Falling forward, exhausted, over Ajit's corpse he felt the hot sun on the back of his neck. Parched, he lifted his head, pulled his arms out from under the body and stood up. His hands were covered in blood. As he looked at the gruesome sight his heart palpitated wildly. He felt nausea and disgust. He looked at his bloody hands in horror and plunged them deep into the sand, vigorously rubbing them clean as if his sanity depended on it. When he pulled them out they were tinted pink. He flattened the tent and threw it over the corpse. It lay on the golden sand like a piece of discarded litter, black and bulky. As he stared at it the concealed corpse took on a grotesque form in his imagination and became even more frightening. He trembled. The images faded. Bizarrely, the shroud suddenly seemed disrespectful. He grabbed the tent and yanked it away. Ajit's body looked peaceful and his expression serene. Inexplicably, he was overwhelmed with a feeling of calm. He straightened the tent into a square and slowly and reverently laid Ajit's body on it. He drank the last of the water and waited for death. 'Come quickly,' he muttered, 'I am ready.' Looking up to the horizon he saw in the haze the blurry outline of a black rider. Ah, death is here, he thought. He knelt in the sand and watched, mesmerised, as the shape rode towards him. This is either death itself, or my executioner, he thought. He hallucinated that he could hear the bells of a submerged cathedral. As the apparition neared he squinted, his mind and emotions completely open, waiting. Now the camel and rider were over him, the camel vivid and alive; he could see it, smell it and he could hear it roar. He trusted his senses suddenly; this was a living thing hovering over him.

'Thank God I am not too late for you!' He recognised Sofia's soft melodious voice.

He thought maybe, for a moment, his senses had tricked him and that he was dreaming. She commanded her camel to kneel. Dressed in black, only her oval face was uncovered, lined and troubled. Dismounting she handed Stefano her leather water carrier. He hesitated for a moment taking her in; greedily he threw the liquid nectar down his throat and over his face. He noticed a second camel attached with a rope. Sofia knelt over Ajit.

'We must bury him quickly and move on before midday,' she said in a voice that was both commanding and remorseful. She stood, went to the camel, rummaged in the satchel, removed two wooden bowls and handed him one. 'Come on, we must dig.' Stefano stood there immobile. She stared gravely and intensely into his face and scrutinised it with a perplexed expression. 'Come on. What is wrong with you? You are in a dream.' She thrust the bowl at him. Reluctantly, he took it. She knelt down in the sand, and with her forehead furrowed and her lips pursed she dug with a gritty determination. She hardly seemed like the same woman. It was incongruous; she was too feminine and pure to be doing such a gruesome task; sinking down on his knees beside her their eyes met, hers challenging. 'Help me,' she said. Tentatively he picked up the bowl and started to dig. He felt the smooth wood and his hands dry and the sun harsh on his skin and his knees penetrating the sand and his back ache. Slowly, reality returned. He gazed at her in awe. She was his rescuer, a beautiful apparition and he felt overwhelming gratitude.

'Which way is East?' said Stefano.

Sofia pointed. 'Over there. Why do you ask?'

'Let's bury him facing the rising sun; he was always up at dawn.'

They moved their positions and dug.

'How did you know to come here?' he said at last.

'Malik returned with three camels, a bloodstained robe and a European compass.'

'He knows you're here?'

'No, I left unseen. The other men are all away.'

'You took a risk.'

'And found you alive. Now I will guide you to Basbereket so you can continue your journey by bus.'

Fine sand like dust floated around them. Sofia's face was white and ghostly against her black hijab, her dark eyes deep and haunting. Soon they had created a sizeable pit. Sofia sat back and studied him, considering.

'You have never buried anybody before.'

'No.'

'The first time is the worst. I have buried two of my children with my bare hands like this, in the sand. My three year old daughter Thurayya, and then my stillborn son Dawud.'

'I'm sorry,' said Stefano.

'Ajit was too good to live. It is written. Now you must take his place,' said Sofia.

Stefano sighed. 'Not me. It would take me a lifetime to reach his level of spiritual maturity, if at all.'

'Then you must start now. Do you have a more important task in life?'

'No.'

'You are inexperienced in the ways of the world and lack confidence, but I sense strength in you.'

Stefano looked at her in silence.

'With each hard lesson we mature. When they died Thurayya and Dawud gave me a gift. Thurayya gave me compassion and Dawud gave me resourcefulness. I wonder what gift Ajit has given you.'

She looked strangely mysterious suddenly with her white face and her black fathomless eyes. There was an odd feeling in his belly and a constriction in his throat. She was suddenly mother and lover rolled into one. He wanted to hold her, to be comforted like a child and at the same time clasp her breasts and smooth his hands along the soft contours of her hips and her belly. Her lips were slightly parted; he looked into the dark hollow of her mouth. He swallowed hard and came to.

'I only feel pain.'

'Be patient and the gift will become clear.'

'Like this, life is brutal.'

'One moment we are alive, the next dead. This is the way of the world. The great mystery.'

Stefano felt the agony of grief radiate out from his solar plexus to every cell in his body, and he shuddered, tears pouring down his cheeks. Ashamed, he put his face in his hands and sobbed.

'You are a man. Do not cry like a woman.' Sofia's voice was steady and commanding. 'There will be time for tears later. Now we must be practical. Remember the gift.' Stefano sat upright and breathed deeply. He felt a tidal wave of love for this enigmatic and audacious woman that made him almost breathless. 'The pit is big enough now. We must put him in. Here, you take his arms.'

Sofia took his legs. Gently they eased Ajit's body into the pit. Sitting back on their knees on either side of the pit they looked at the body, stiff and lifeless and covered in a thin film of dust.

'Do you have any prayers for him?' said Sofia.

Stefano shook his head. 'My mind is blank, I can't remember anything; you use your prayer.'

'I have a Sufi prayer.'

'Any prayer will do for Ajit, as long as it is said authentically.'

Sofia closed her eyes and with arms outstretched recited an Arabic prayer. She took some grains of sand between her thumb and forefinger and with exquisite gracefulness sprinkled them into the pit. With a voice like a dove she sang a poignant lament. 'Now we bury him,' she said softly. With both palms she pushed sand down onto Ajit's body. Stefano did the same. Soon Ajit was covered.

'Come, get on the camel. Take the compass.' She reached into the pocket of her gown and pulled it out. As she placed it in his hand he felt the smoothness of her skin and gentleness of her touch. Their eyes met briefly. He savoured the moment. They got on the camels and rode across the desert, side by side.

When they arrived at Basbereket he said, 'You are the most beautiful and courageous woman I have ever met.'

'Are you flattering me?'

Stefano felt as if a knife had pierced his heart. 'I only say what I feel.'

Sofia studied him for a moment.

'Forgive me, I should have known that. I can see that now. You speak from the heart. My husband has many visitors; most of them are sycophants and liars.' She sighed. 'I am too cynical. It is only with Sufis that I feel safe.'

'I forgive you.'

'I am no better than the next woman and you no worse than the next man. Both of us struggle and do what we can, but you have an inner strength.'

'I will remember what you have said. I will be worthy, if not of Ajit, of you.'

'Be worthy of Ajit,' said Sofia as she met and held his gaze.

'Have a safe journey,' said Stefano.

'I will; the desert is my friend... and you... take care. So... until we meet again.'

She smiled and in the smile there was a flash of genuine and sincere feeling. He stood and watched her for a long time as she rode away.

CHAPTER 17

An Lac ashram, Switzerland

Ralph picked up the white envelope from his desk, read his name and smelt a faint perfume. The handwriting was vaporous with a flowerlike grace. He fingered it ponderously for a few moments, put it back down on the desk and picked up his pen.

'They've left Madrid and are on their way back now.' Looking up Ralph saw Maurice standing in the doorway, leaning against the wooden frame. 'Tom did well; brave and resourceful they said.'

'Well, I thought it would either make or break him; he's a man at last I hope.' Ralph threw down his pen and sat back in his chair.

'As they were leaving there was a massive fire; Paradiso was burnt to the ground.'

'The old shopping centre? I thought there were security guards surrounding it 24 hours.'

'An inside job.'

'At war with themselves. Well, well. I wonder what will happen to those people now?'

'There are not many choices if they still want to hold on to their old lifestyle.'

'The remnants of a diseased and dying society, gone up in smoke.' Ralph shook his head, crossed his arms, turned and looked out of the window at the trees billowing in the wind.

'I've got more news, good and bad I'm afraid.'

Ralph swivelled his chair to face Maurice.

'Tell me about it.'

Maurice took a seat.

'The network is growing really fast, far better than we hoped,' said Maurice.

'Go on.'

Maurice turned some pages in his spiral bound notebook. 'Coptic Christian refugees, originally from Egypt, have joined Giovanni's group in northern Italy. In Turkey, Jews and Christians have linked up and formed a resistance movement; very underground. The place is swarming with New Islamists but they're in a strong position; they've got resources. In Hungary, Romania and southern Germany Muslims rejected by Imam Salim - you get rejected by anything there - have joined Magdalena's group... I could go on.'

'Our contacts have done well rallying up support. I thought it'd be impossible to get them to come together like this, didn't you?'

'Not when you know it's been masterminded by our man upstairs.'

'Annando, I haven't seen him for days. I thought he was resting; Sunnido takes his food to his room.'

Maurice laughed. 'You couldn't be more wrong. He seems to have a new lease of life. He writes thirty detailed emails a day.'

Ralph frowned and leaned forwards.

'What's he saying in them?'

'He's trying to get small groups to join into forces. This is the bad news. He's got intelligence that the New Islamists are assembling, planning to attack An Lac. He's organising our strategic defence by getting outside groups to approach, set up and defend us from all directions. It's still in the planning stage: our exact location is still a mystery to everyone outside.'

'So, war is imminent. I thought we'd have more time.' Ralph rubbed his chin. 'How much time have we got?'

'Weeks at the most.'

Ralph sighed. 'How many Pitot devices are in the valley?'

'About a hundred, but we'll need to revamp them and scatter more so wherever the allies arrive from they'll be able to communicate with us. By then I'll have had the blueprint from Erin for the Hanzza hand weapon so we'll be able to put up resistance from here as well.'

'Good, but I didn't think they'd be needed so soon,' said Ralph.

'All the printing stations have been restocked with plenty of raw material, When Erin gets here I want to go into full production of the weapons.'

'Have you thought about what's going to happen when the Hanzzas run out of charge?'

'That's what the Lentas are for; close hand to hand combat.'

'That's the hand weapon you've designed yourself?'

'Yes, it delivers electric shocks through metal spikes sticking out of the barrel. There are three settings. One, the lowest, delivers a high voltage shock; on the highest it will kill; in between it causes brief unconsciousness.'

'How brief?'

'Several hours.'

'Is it ready?'

'Yes, it's fully tested and operational.'

Ralph took a deep breath, 'This is becoming horribly real.'

'I know.' Maurice compressed his lips and his brows contracted.

'So, Annando's a guru, icon and military commander; completely indispensable. Let's hope, for all our sakes, he stays well. What an enigma he is.' Ralph shook his head. 'So when is he planning to brief us all?'

'Just as soon as the plan is in place.'

'He never was good at delegating.'

'What about you? You've enough on your plate. I hope you've been delegating.'

'My work seems like chicken feed compared with Annando's. Yes, I've got enough people to help me.'

'Isabella seems better; perhaps she could run the community again.'

'I don't think she's quite herself yet. Anyway, everyday things seem futile now.'

The telephone rang in the room next door. 'That's him now; he'll be needing something and he doesn't like waiting.'

As Maurice walked away, Ralph stretched himself back in the chair with his hands clasped behind his head. Looking down he saw the white envelope, leant forward, slit it open with his thumb and unfolded the paper. He glanced at the ethereal handwriting then let the letter fall onto the desk. He stood up and walked to the window. For a few moments he looked out, unseeing, lost in thought. With a sigh he walked back to the desk, picked up the letter and began to read.

Dear Ralph,

I am writing you this letter because I didn't want to compromise you by talking to you alone which I know you would find awkward. I have noticed you avoiding me, for good reason, but this hurts me extremely, and I want to explain myself and apologise.

Ralph, I am so sorry for the way I behaved on Sunday. It was inexcusable. I know this sounds cowardly and feeble, but I have not been myself. You know that since Ian went missing I haven't felt well and there's been a craziness about me.

I remember our encounter only dimly, but I do remember that I put you in an impossible position and under immense pressure. Oh, what you must have thought of me! I dread to think; it is too humiliating! You must have wished there was an asylum nearby and you could lock me up, this mad creature.

All credit to you that you were able to hang on with such strength and steadiness and helped to ground me when my behaviour was so bizarre. You never compromised your principles but showed compassion and understanding throughout.

The episode with Tom is something I deeply regret and causes me intense pain and embarrassment to even think of it. I just hope that in the fullness of time Tom will have the maturity to look at it dispassionately and see it as an isolated incident that happened in a time of extreme pressure when I was not myself. I hope this will not affect our relationship in the long run. He is only a boy, although a little headstrong, I know. I apologise for my inappropriate behaviour with Tom.

I am pleased to say that I am quite myself now and those feelings I had are completely in check. I am, and always will be, a Brahma Kumari set on a life of purity and devotion and this episode is simply an opportunity for learning, as Annando calls every setback, which will make me stronger.

I have always admired you, more so now because you behaved towards me with such understanding, patience and restraint. You are so strong. No one could have had a better friend. Please forgive me Ralph, I want nothing more than for us to be as we were, dear friends, although I know I cannot turn the clock back. I hope you can find it in your heart to forgive me and that we can now move on.

Your steadfast and penitent friend,
Isabella.

Ralph hesitated for a moment, folded the paper, put it back in the envelope and slid it into his back pocket.

*

At 3.00pm Ralph made his way to the small meeting room. Entering, he saw Annando alone, sat in a chair looking out of the window towards the mountains. Annando turned and beckoned Ralph to sit next to him.

'You, Ralph, have been with me since the beginning and have a deep understanding and commitment to your spiritual path. Everyone here trusts and respects you. You are my natural successor. I want you to take over when the time comes.'

Ralph swallowed hard and frowned.

'I am honoured and impressed with your confidence in me, but I am not sure I am ready.'

'Not ready? Some people will never be ready; you are not one of them,' Annando's expression was kind and sincere.

'I am sorry to let you down, but sadly, I am not ready.'

Annando looked at him for a long time. 'I sense that you are troubled. Do you want to tell me what it is?'

'It is nothing I can't work through, given time, lots of time.'

'Hmm, Isabella?'

Ralph took a deep breath; he felt paralysed for a moment.

Annando touched him reassuringly on the shoulder. 'I respect your decision,' he said quietly, 'and your need to give this some more thought.' Slowly he got up and walked out of the room.

Ralph rubbed his chin and heard the rasp of his bristles. How does he do it, he thought emphatically. I know he's not clairvoyant, but how does he do it? He always knows.

CHAPTER 18

'Annando, I want to tell you something.'

Annando stopped walking. 'What is it, Tom?'

'People are praising me but they don't know the whole story. I don't deserve praise.' He tried whispering but could still hear his voice reverberate off the stone walls of the corridor.

'Why is that?'

'I used someone.' Tom looked away.

'Whom did you use?' said Annando quietly.

'A girl. I pretended I was interested in her to get information about the prison, then I dumped her.'

'And how does that make you feel?'

'Guilty and sorry.' Tom glanced up, Annando looked steadily at him. 'But I justified it to myself at the time; I was so determined to make Dad proud of me.'

'Hmm, you have awareness and a conscience. What have you learnt?'

'That lies feel bad.'

'Are you going to tell your father the truth?'

'I don't know.'

'He may respect you more if you do.'

Tom bit his lip and looked up. Annando's face was full of compassion and Tom felt a sudden surge of love and respect for him.

'Think about it.' Annando paused for a moment. 'You are resourceful and have a quick mind. In your dealings with others use more skilful means and do not exploit the innocent.'

'Yes. Thank you.'

Tom felt the light reassuring touch of Annando's hand on his shoulder and the warmth of his smile. Annando turned. Tom watched him walk the length of the corridor, his stick gently tapping the floor. How lucky I've been growing up in this ashram, he thought.

*

Stefano threw himself to his knees and cupped his calloused hands around Annando's warm ankles. For a moment everything went spinning and his heart throbbed. His head bent, tears gushed on to the straps of Annando's sandals. He sobbed, aware only of the force of his own emotions and the thin threadbare straps, now wet.

'I've failed, I've let you down,' he gasped.

'You did what you could. There was nothing more you could have done.' Annando's voice was soft and reassuring.

'I should have protected him.'

'There were powerful forces at work.'

'As he was dying, Ajit asked me to tell you his death was not in vain.'

'Let's hope not. In the fullness of time we'll see. Take some time to recover and come and see me when you feel better,' said Annando quietly.

'But I've failed.'

He heard Annando sigh.

'Get up.' Annando's voice was louder.

Stefano released his hands and saw the skin on Annando's ankles red where he had clenched them; he pushed back on his knees and stood in front of Annando.

'Who was it who sent you?' said Annando. Stefano swallowed hard when he saw Annando's eyes full of pain.

CHAPTER 19

Ralph pulled the front door behind him and it clicked shut.

'Had a good day?' Jane undid the tie behind her back and pulled the apron over her head.

'Busy. Do you really want to know what I've done?'

'Yes, of course,' she said tenderly. 'I'm always interested in what you do.'

She seems in a good mood today thought Ralph as he flopped into the armchair.

'I've cleaned the whole chicken barn, that was a back breaking job by itself. Collected around three hundred eggs, swept the chimney, mended a hole in the roof of the Swartz's bungalow, tested fifty Pitot devices for Maurice and other tasks.' He sighed. 'Just an ordinary day.'

'You're tired, poor Ralph, always so much to do.'

'Always, but it's all *seva*, done with an open heart however grubby the task.'

'Yes, it's the same for me.'

'What about you?'

'I've got on with my chores as usual. I was surprised by something though.' Jane frowned. 'I was about to put your trousers in the washing machine, well, I always check the pockets, and I found this letter.' She held up a white envelope. 'I thought it might be important.'

Ralph noticed Isabella's writing.

'No, it's nothing. Can I have it please?' Ralph stretched out his arm.

Jane clutched it tight and stared at him. 'It's from Isabella.'

'You read it.' Ralph felt himself stiffen. 'Why? It's mine!' He got up, facing her.

'I was curious, especially when she mentioned Sunday last week, the day you behaved so strangely, so full of passion and later regret. I didn't understand, then.'

Ralph took a deep breath, 'You have no right to read my letter.'

'As soon as I read it, it made sense, the way you'd behaved.' Her eyes bored into him. 'She'd roused your passion!'

Ralph took a few deep breaths and came out in a sweat.

'Look, it was nothing. If you must know I was inside cleaning the chimney when she ducked under the lintel and almost threw herself at me. She was completely wild! It has nothing to do with us.'

'She said you resisted her.'

'Of course I did.'

'Don't you find me attractive any more?' Jane pulled her long plait over her shoulder and played with it, looking coyly at him.

'You know how I'm trying to live.'

'You found her attractive, so attractive that you couldn't control yourself. She was out of bounds, but not me, your wife, I was available.' Her voice began to crack. 'So you came home to make love to me whilst you were thinking only of her!' Jane blinked, her eyes filled with tears and she whimpered.

Ralph took a pace towards her but she put up her hand and backed towards the sink. He felt a lump in his throat. 'I'm sorry that's how it seems,' he said quietly.

'You deceived me and used me. What you did was despicable!' Jane's voice rang and snapped.

'I didn't do anything with Isabella.'

'But you wanted to.' She wiped her face with her hankie.

'I didn't pursue her, believe me.'

'You used me! I've thought about this, I've thought about almost nothing else since I found the letter. When we made love you weren't even there. Your body was there but all your desire and thoughts were about Isabella.'

'You can't read my mind; you don't know what I was thinking.'

She looked at him with a mixture of pain, anger and disappointment and he felt nauseous. 'But I know you weren't with me.'

'I messed up! I made a mistake!'

Jane shook her head and gave him an anguished look.

'Even Annando was married once as a young man and had a son. You're trying so hard to be perfect and look how far you fall. Lilies that fester smell far worse than weeds.'

'Forgive me. I love you. I'll earn your trust again.' He looked into her eyes.

'Then do that, Ralph, you do that.' Jane threw the envelope at him, rushed out of the house and slammed the door.

Ralph felt his body tremble; he took a deep breath, slowly bent down and picked up the envelope from the floor. He felt the flimsy paper between his fingers. It was now grubby and creased and smelling of washing-up liquid. He read it, tore the paper into smaller and smaller pieces and threw them in the bin.

'Damn!' he said.

CHAPTER 20

'Our intelligence shows New Islamist armies mustering and making their way to An Lac,' said Ralph. He looked at the others who were standing in sombre silence round the table.

'So the rumours are true?' said Carlos.

'I'm afraid so.'

'What sort of numbers are we talking about and when and where are they coming from?' Carlos said, scrutinising the electronic map of Switzerland set in the table.

'Let's zoom out.' As Maurice ran his finger across the glass from the centre to the outside of the table, the scale decreased showing Switzerland nestling between the countries of Europe.

'This is what we know so far: Ali's forces will be coming up from the south west through Grenoble and along the 203 across to Megeve.' Ralph pointed at the map. 'Mahdi has a smaller force coming from Luxemburg and Strasbourg via the E27; Salim, who controls Germany and the Czech Republic, will be approaching from the E62 from the northeast and Jalal Kowi from the south east along the E25.'

'Are these roads still passable?' said Carlos.

'They are all major routes and passable until we sabotage them.'

'So, what sort of numbers?' Carlos rubbed his chin.

'Hundreds.'

'We're completely outnumbered, we can't possibly win,' said Carlos.

'Not so,' said Annando. He stood up and walked over to the map. 'History has shown that it is more important to outwit your enemy than to outfight him. They may have force in numbers and weaponry but we have more subtle weapons.'

Erin pushed her hair behind her ears, 'Please explain.'

'We are not seeking to destroy our Muslim brothers but to win them over; not all of them are fanatical fundamentalists. On the battlefield there is no victory for anybody, only suffering. Our goal is to remove their will to fight.'

'We are not even using lethal weapons; the battle isn't equal. We're sitting ducks,' said Raphael.

'You can only kill the duck if you can find it. They know we're near Martigny, but our intelligence suggests that's all they know. With luck they will not find An Lac until we're ready. We must outwit them with surprise, deception and regular harassment. We have to undermine their morale and their willingness to do us harm.'

'So what's the plan?' said Carlos.

'Maurice, please demonstrate,' Ralph said.

Maurice ran his finger towards the centre of the table and stopped when the relief showed An Lac and surrounding mountains. 'As you know we've had Pitot devices in the valley for months now monitoring any unusual movement.'

'How many are there?' asked Erin.

'About three hundred spread over an area of five miles,' said Ralph. 'When the New Islamists approach, the devices detect their movement, estimate how many troops are in the valley and alert us here. Some have cameras so we'll be able to get some pictures, but we'll send out scouts as well to watch them and monitor their numbers and behaviour.'

Isabella frowned. 'What good does that do if we have no troops of our own?'

'But we have. As we speak there are small groups of allies on their way here. You know for weeks now we've been sending groups out to clean up the mountain ranger cottages and the hides. You thought this was a waste of time?' said Ralph.

'Yes, completely, I know, I've been doing it,' said Tom.

'These places across the valleys are where the allies are going to hide, spy on the Muslims and run ambushes and skirmishes.'

'Clever,' said Raphael,' so we're not going to face them in battle?'

'Not until we must,' said Annando. 'We must use the advantage of high ground and steep terrain. Even the allies won't know the exact position of An Lac but each will be given a strategic area to attack from and defend. When they get here we must make sure they have food, shelter, medical supplies and everything else they need. They will be briefed and each group given our full support. They must learn the complex routes through the mountain passes and forests and will need a guide from here to stay with them. But the command of each small group will remain with that leader and not with our guide.'

'So each leader will decide how and when to strike,' said Erin.

'Exactly so,' Annando wobbled ever so slightly then placed his hands on the edge of the table, 'because they will have the advantage of knowing the behaviour of the group of Muslims they're targeting.'

'But they will be advised by our intelligence from here at An Lac; the master plan will be co-ordinated from here,' said Ralph.

Isabella came and stood next to Annando. 'Shall I bring a chair over. You look tired,' she said.

'No, I am fine standing,' said Annando, pulling himself upright with a visible physical effort, 'but thank you for asking.'

'So who is the overall commander?' said Isabella softly and she looked at each of them in turn.

'I am,' said Annando decisively, 'with Ralph as my second-in-command. We will confuse the Muslims, draw them in then surprise them with an attack where they are weakest, deplete their forces and demoralise them.'

'But with the Hanzzas and Lentas on stun they're just going to get up and fight again, whereas we will be killed,' said Isabella. 'We are the ones being demoralised surely.'

'The North Vietnamese lost moral ground in the TET offensive in 1968 because afterwards they were brutal. They massacred innocent south Vietnamese government officials and thirty Christian nuns. I remember it well,' Annando said solemnly. 'Let's see what happens when they realise we have not shed blood.'

'I don't want to fight at all,' said Isabella.

'You are needed here to run the community,' said Annando. 'Is there anyone else who doesn't want to fight?'

'I am ready to fight and defend An Lac. I'd like to be a guide and teach the allies the routes through the forests,' said Tom.

'And me,' said Stefano.

'Good.' Annando looked around. 'Any other volunteers?'

'Raphael and I are ready,' said Carlos. 'Tell us what to do.'

'Someone needs to stay here in the control room,' said Erin.

'Annando and I will be here as well as Maurice who'll be monitoring the equipment,' said Ralph.

'Wouldn't it make sense for us to move our HQ to another location if the New Islamists discover where we are and try to raid us?' Erin asked.

Maurice shook his head. 'That's difficult with the equipment set up as it is.'

'That will be the end stage,' Annando said gravely. 'We will put off any direct large scale military confrontation for as long as possible. Let's see if we can outwit, rather than outfight, Ali and the others first.'

Sunnido stood in the doorway and knocked on the open door, 'Annando, you need your medication urgently.'

'I will come.'

Annando picked up his stick and shuffled towards the doorway. They watched as he left with Sunnido close behind and listened in silence to the tap of Annando's stick as it died away.

Isabella frowned. 'I've never heard Sunnido call Annando for his medication before. That worries me.'

'Nor have I.' Ralph rubbed his chin.

'It confirms what I've suspected all along,' said Erin, 'he's living on borrowed time.'

'Maybe we all are,' said Ralph.

'This is suicide!' exclaimed Raphael. 'What experience does Annando have of military strategy?'

'As a young man Annando was in Vietnam during the Vietnam War, but he never talks about it,' said Erin.

'Annando speaks with authority; I think he knows what he's doing,' said Carlos.

Raphael scratched his ear. 'Perhaps he's hiding something.'

Ralph gave a short laugh. 'Ha, Annando will only ever tell you what you need to know.'

Isabella picked a hankie out of her pocket, blew her nose and wept softly, 'Annando always knows best, but we must protect him. He is the only hope for the future. There will only be me, Ralph and Maurice here. If they come it won't be enough.'

'When the time comes Annando won't want protection, believe me, wait and see,' said Ralph.

CHAPTER 21

Stefano took a step back and looked at the man he had struck on the head, who writhed like a snake on the ground. All around him the battle raged with the clash of metal and plastic, the sizzle of electricity and the shouts and groans of men and women lunging at each other with Lenta, sword, baton and stones. The drizzle falling from the murky sky cooled him. The trampled grass was now a dirty brown and strewn with bodies, dead and unconscious, although it was difficult to tell which was which. There was an acrid smell of blood and sweat that he could taste at the back of his mouth. His eyes darted back and forth. Who's next? he thought. There, some twenty metres away, was a Muslim in a sleek white robe and black head wrap pulling his blood-stained sword out of a man's chest. In a flash he saw that there was something familiar about the man's height and posture. As the Muslim stood up and gazed in his direction Stefano gasped, the hairs on his skin stood on end; he felt a shudder of anger and adrenalin flow through him. As Stefano approached, the man recognised him and his eyes narrowed.

'Ah, Ajit's minder! So we meet again and I see you are not yet dead,' said Malik.

'Now is my turn for revenge.'

Malik smirked, 'With that primitive club, imbecile?'

'It may look primitive, but I wield it!' said Stefano, lunging at Malik.

Malik lifted his sword and the weapons clashed: Stefano threw his weight forward and forced Malik to step back. He could see Malik's eyes as dark as night and as remorseless as on that fateful day in the desert. Stefano's hate and determination welled up; his hands burned feverishly, his face smouldered hot, his heart palpitated wildly. Roaring like an animal, he felt a rush of superhuman energy as if he were in the 'zone' where anything was within his grasp. He stepped forwards and with lightning speed brought his Lenta down onto Malik's shoulder. With the contact there was a sizzle. With a cry of pain Malik stumbled backwards.

'So, you imbecile, you have found some courage.'

'Hurts, does it?' said Stefano.

Malik straightened up, 'Not as much as this will,' and raised his sword again.

With the speed of a striking cobra Stefano struck him on the hip. Malik fell to his knees, sank forward and let go of the sword. Stefano struck him on the back and on the arm and on the head over and over again and kicked him with his boot in the thigh and the shoulder. 'Suffer, animal, you are not important enough to die!' With each blow he felt a surge of pleasure overwhelm him.

'Stop! Have you learned nothing in the last twenty years?'

Stefano looked up. Erin stood over him panting, her eyes blazing.

'He's the one who murdered Ajit,' hissed Stefano.

'Gandhi said "an eye for an eye makes the whole world blind".'

Her face was red and sheened with sweat, her hair bedraggled, her clothes dirty and rank, her Lenta loose in her hand.

'But he killed Ajit and left me for dead.'

'Please, please, no more. Mercy,' said Malik in a hoarse gasping voice. He sat back on his haunches, his face pale and frightened with parted lips and staring, terrified eyes, his hands in prayer.

'Look at him now; he's a pathetic coward, a little man,' said Erin.

'What would you have me do? What do we do with scum like this?' shrieked Stefano.

'He needs to answer for his crimes, but not like this.'

'How then?'

'We'll tie him up, deal with him later. Here, help me.'

She stood behind Malik, pulled his arms behind his back, secured his wrists with plastic ties from her pocket and stood him up. 'Come on, let's walk him to An Lac and lock him up.'

'You walk him to An Lac,' said Stefano. He pulled a handkerchief from his pocket, wiped his face on it and used it to tightly blindfold Malik, 'I've got more important battles to fight,' and spat on the ground.

'Take control of yourself; do not be overwhelmed,' shouted Erin as she watched him go.

Erin led Malik up through the forest. She pushed him into a hut, locked the door and made her way to An Lac. Exhausted, she burst through the French doors into the control room. Annando, Maurice, Ralph and Jane were leaning over the map lit up like a slot machine with lights flashing.

'What news, Erin?' said Ralph.

'It's not good out there,' said Erin, breathless. She flopped down with her back against a wall and her legs straight. 'Stefano found the man who murdered Ajit. We captured him. I've locked him in a hut down the hill.'

'What do you plan to do with him?' Annando said softly.

'I don't really know. Stefano was killing him and it just seemed wrong somehow. Malik is a murderer and he must pay for that, but killing him seems wrong.'

'There's a battle going on out there, people are dying all around,' said Annando.

'But this was more than that. Stefano was full of hate, he wanted revenge.'

'Ajit's murder stirred strong emotions in all of us. It is justice that is needed. What does your conscience tell you to do?'

'Leave him until we can deal with him, when all this is finished.'

Erin tilted her head back against the wall, closed her eyes and sighed. In the distance she heard the shouts and clash of battle.

'Very well,' said Annando, 'let's leave him for now.'

'What's the news from the control centre?' she said and opened her eyes.

'Not good, now the battle has spilled out into the valley. There are too many of them, we are not warriors and they're brutal,' said Ralph.

'Not all of them,' said Maurice, 'there are glimmers of hope, a small number have come round from unconsciousness and refused to fight again: twenty of Imam Mahdi's forces have come over to us.'

Erin noticed Isabella standing in a corner with her head bowed and her arms tightly crossed.

'Twenty, that's hope of a kind, I suppose. So what now?' asked Erin.

Carlos marched in, his face red and burning with intensity; he propped himself up against a wall. 'It's Ali,' he said breathlessly, 'he's too strong, his men are getting up again and again; we're being slaughtered. With him inspiring them we're finished.'

'And Jalal Kowi's army haven't even got here yet to finish us off,' whispered Maurice, shaking his head.

'Anyway, we've got to recharge. I need a battery then I'm going back,' said Carlos.

'Here, take one.' Maurice handed him a fresh battery. Carlos left by the French windows.

'These people are not spiritually mature enough for non-violence,' said Annando despondently. He walked towards the French windows and looked down into the valley.

A shrill beep pierced the silence. 'It's Raphael!' Maurice pressed a button and the line crackled.

'There's an enormous army, men dressed in white approaching from the E25.' Raphael's voice was faint and distorted.

'Jalal Kowi,' said Maurice and took a deep breath. 'How many?'

'Hundreds.'

Isabella squealed, put her hand over her mouth and wept quietly. They listened to more crackle.

'Wait, there's a scout out front on a horse; he's talking to Tom,' said Raphael.

Annando turned around and looked intently at Maurice.

'Tom? How the hell did Tom get there?' said Ralph.

They fell silent and stood motionless, listening.

'Tom's coming up the hill towards me, there's a man with him and another following... leading a horse.'

'Stupid boy, it's a trap,' said Ralph, clutching the table so hard his knuckles became white.

The line crackled again, Tom's voice came through. 'Jalal Kowi's here; he wants to speak to Annando. Is Annando there?'

Annando raised his head and stood still for a moment, considering. 'I am Annando, what have you to say?'

'Malik killed your representative in my name. Nobody kills in my name.' The distant voice was resolute, strong and rich. 'Ajit was right about the other imams. Brothers, my fellow Muslims and I will fight the lesser jihad against those who would corrupt Mohammed's teachings. Those who call themselves Muslims but whose hearts are insincere.' They heard a horse neigh. 'We are here to join forces with our mystic brothers and fight Ali's armies so that Mohammed's true message may be lived authentically. This is the will of Allah!'

Ralph saw Annando's face soften. 'We thank you for making this life-giving choice,' he said. 'I will come to meet you.'

'It will be my pleasure to meet you at last,' said Jalal Kowi. There was some more crackle, then silence.

'Annando, you can't mean it?' Isabella's voice held a trace of fear.

Annando turned towards Maurice, his hand outstretched. 'Give me a Lenta: I may need to fight my way through.'

Maurice shook his head. 'You need to stay here where we can protect you.'

'Please Annando, don't.' Isabella rushed towards him.

'I do not need protection,' said Annando.

Isabella burst into tears, fell at his feet and grabbed his orange robe in her hand.

'Please don't,' she sobbed, 'you will be recognised and killed.'

Annando stood still, his hand outstretched. 'The Lenta,' he said, looking at Maurice.

Maurice looked towards Ralph.

'I will go with Annando,' said Ralph.

'No, I will,' briskly Erin stood up. 'You're needed to take charge here, Ralph.'

Maurice unlocked a cupboard and gently placed a Lenta in Annando's hand.

'Thank you,' said Annando.

Annando carefully slung the Lenta's strap over his shoulder and with his stick in one hand walked to the open door, on to the path and down the hill with Erin close by.

'I will not leave Annando,' said Isabella, hurrying behind.

'Where's your Lenta? You're on your own: I'm not looking after you as well,' said Erin.

They followed a narrow path parallel to the field of battle.

'Annando, we are exposed here, we need to take another path,' said Erin.

'No, I need to meet Jalal Kowi as soon as possible and this is the quickest route,' said Annando and strode on.

They came to where the path opened out into the battlefield.

'Come, it is only a small distance,' said Annando, leading the way along the side of the field.

The cacophony of clashing, banging and groaning was almost deafening. As they briskly moved on a gruff husky tenor voice shouted from behind, 'There's Annando, kill him!'

They turned around. Isabella screamed. Erin stood in front of Annando brandishing her Lenta. 'Don't come any closer!' she said baring her teeth. The man was much bigger than her and the fight unequal; he grabbed her arm, pushed her away like a puppet and lunged at Annando's torso with a knife. Annando stumbled and fell backwards onto the ground, his hands clutching his stomach. An ally charged at the man from behind, struck him hard on the head and he fell unconscious. Whimpering, Isabella rushed to Annando, squatted down and nestled his head in her lap. Three allies gathered round.

'Is that really Annando?' said one of them, panting.

'Yes, we must get him back up the hill,' said Erin, 'help me.'

Tenderly they carried him back to the control room. With trembling hands Isabella laid blankets on the ground and they gently placed him on them. Sunnido examined the wound, looked up and shook his head slightly. Ralph felt his throat swell and his chest tighten.

'I need to go to Jalal Kowi,' said Annando in a feeble voice.

'We will get a message to him,' said Ralph.

'Tell him I will come later. How are things?' said Annando. 'The truth.'

'Jalal Kowi's troops are on the battlefield now but...'
Ralph suppressed the spasm in his voice.

'But what?'

'Ali's men are giving no quarter.'

Annando looked up at the ceiling in thoughtful stillness.
'Do what you must to end this bloodshed,' he said quietly.

Ralph sat back on his heels, grasped by a feeling of
providence. He was silent in contemplation for a moment, 'I
will take on this burden,' he said, stood up and walked to
the French windows.

'Be careful,' said Jane. She grabbed his hand and looked
deep into his eyes. He felt the warmth of her breath on his
cheek.

Taking a Lenta in his hand he strode down the hill
towards the battlefield. He waded through the sea of
fighting men and women. Ralph saw Ali, dressed in black,
wielding a sword in each hand and shouting, 'Death to the
infidels!' As Ralph approached for some unfathomable
reason he felt no fear, only the rightness of the inevitability
of the confrontation.

Ralph stood still and watched Ali. Ali turned and saw
him. For some moments they confronted each other in
silence.

'So who are you, standing there so calm, so serene?' said
Ali and spat. 'You're too young to be Annando.'

Ali's eyes were black holes brimming with depravity, his
teeth bared like a wild animal, exposing his pink gums.

'Annando is a much greater man than I. I am his
representative.'

'So, you are one of the mystics.'

'Some people like to call us that.'

'And what do you want?'

'I want to end this bloodshed.'

'So do I, you misguided pacifist. When you are all dead
it will end!' Raising his sword Ali lunged at Ralph.

Ralph aimed his Lenta, and as if time had stood still, at the last moment he hesitated, then switched the control from stun to kill. In Ralph's head there was only a vague distant echo of battle, and a strange reality, as if everything moved in slow motion. He saw Ali's sword flash in the sunlight aimed towards his heart. Driven by what seemed like forces unseen he brought the Lenta down on Ali's head. As the Lenta made contact he felt a sudden piercing pain through his body as if he had taken on the karma of a thousand dead men. Suddenly there was the clash, bang, ring, scream of battle, the smell of blood and the sight of carnage. Ali lay writhing on the wet earth, twitched and was still, limp and lifeless. Ralph backed away and watched as Muslims gathered around the body. Ralph strode briskly back up the hill.

'It's finished,' he said, breathless, as he leant against the French windows.

'You have done enough; you are the best of men.' He felt Jane's warm arms around him, soothing, reassuring and the familiar smell of washing-up liquid. 'I have always loved and respected you, my dear Ralph.'

He smiled weakly at her. Looking up he saw the room now half full of people, some with their backs to the walls standing in sombre silence, some squatting and kneeling around Annando. Several were weeping quietly. He knelt next to Annando.

Marurice's voice, low and mellow, pierced the silence. 'The fighting is slowing. I've lost audio but I've got a video here from Ahmed. It's a bit fuzzy but I can make out... there are children on the battlefield, groups of two and three.' People looked round, staring intently at Maurice. 'The girls are giving out flowers and the boys are carrying jugs of water and giving cups to the Muslims who've begun to sit up.'

Jane, Adeena and three other women rushed up and peered intently at the screen.

'Oh God, they're ashram children,' said Jane, 'there's Anton and John and Simon, and there's...'

'That's Venus and Bruno, even little Aseem; we must stop them, they'll be harmed,' said Adeena.

'Wait, they're not being harmed,' said Maurice, 'they're accepting it, look.'

'Who told them to do that?' said Jane.

'I don't know.' Adeena looked up and around the room, 'did anyone here?'

There was silence.

'Then how?' said Jane frowning.

'When someone is sick or dying they always bring flowers and water,' said Isabella, cradling Annando's head in her lap. 'This is all they know; you must know that.'

'Look,' said Maurice peering at the screen, 'nobody is fighting any more.'

Ralph watched Annando slowly open his eyes and smile faintly, 'Leave the children,' he whispered.

Jalal Kowi, Sofia, Carlos and a group of children pushed inside from the open windows and stood quietly; the room fell silent.

Ralph saw Annando's mouth move. He was deathly pale, going whiter by the moment, his eyes open but glazed. Ralph took a deep breath; a sudden rush of emotion overwhelmed him.

'You need a new leader,' whispered Annando.

'What did he say?' Erin said, straining to hear from her position at Annando's feet.

'We need a new leader,' repeated Ralph.

Ralph leant gently over Annando. 'Who is it to be?

'Look to the future,' whispered Annando.

Ralph took a deep breath and sat back on his heels.

'What did he say?' said Erin.

'Look to the future,' repeated Ralph, his eyes filled with tears.

Across the room people looked at each other in silence.

'Father.' Tilly took a step forward and stood in an empty space; they all looked towards her. 'We have already chosen.' She stepped back and grasped Carlos' hand.

'Me?' Carlos' eyes widened. 'This is unexpected,' he said.

Silently the children in the room gathered around Carlos, grasping his other hand, his belt, his waist. Ralph nodded, 'A good choice,' he said and looked back down at Annando who lay perfectly still, his expression serene, his eyes glazed and empty.

Erin covered her mouth and started to sob. Isabella leaned forward. With an ethereal smile she stretched out her hand and closed Annando's eyes. Slowly and respectfully the group around Annando dispersed as the children encircled his body with wild flowers. Soon the women started chanting a melancholy raga, 'Om Namah Shivaya,' over and over again.

*

'What does the chant mean?' said Jalal Kowi quietly as he stood with Ralph in the fresh air outside.

'I honour the unknowable reality within me.'

'Unknowable?'

'That which I cannot comprehend but I can experience,' said Ralph.

'Ah,' Jalal Kowi nodded. 'I am too late, but I am not too late to share in his legacy. Carlos must give a speech... to everyone,' he said as he spread his arms wide with a flourish.

'Yes, soon,' said Ralph.

Inside the room Erin rocked back and forth, frightened by the intensity of her own emotions, the knot in her throat, the tightness in her chest, her own terrifying wail; she felt as if her whole being would explode with grief. She was aware of the others moving like grey shadows around her, gently, tenderly. She looked up at Isabella, beautiful and serene; she watched the gracious movements of her slim arms as she bathed Annando's corpse with tepid water.

'How are you so peaceful?' said Erin.

'I have mentally rehearsed this hundreds of times,' said Isabella, with liquid eyes flowing with love.

'You are stronger than I.'

'Not stronger, just different.' Isabella's voice sounded ethereal, its effect soothing.

Erin got up and walked down the hill. On a platform overlooking the valley Jalal Kowi, Sofia, Ralph and Carlos were in deep conversation and the hundreds of people in the valley were gathering round, allies, Muslims, children. The dead were being taken away and, once laid out, the children gently placed flowers around them. Time passed but Erin didn't know how long. She stood there as if in a dream.

'Attention!' came a booming voice which snapped her back into the moment. 'Ali is dead and his followers are a spent force,' said Jalal Kowi speaking into a megaphone. 'Look around you at your brothers and sisters. Despite colour, or culture or language or ethnicity, one human family. Look into the eyes of the person standing next to you whether he be Asian, Arab, Caucasian or anything else and see your own image. As Mohammed said in his final sermon, "Humans are formed of many tribes and nations. We are not here to convert, terrorise, fight, oppress or occupy, but to get to know one another."' Jalal Kowi paused for a moment and then resumed. 'Annando is also dead but his ideals live on. An Lac has been a beacon of light in these troubled times, working for the betterment of all of us. Now let us hear from their new leader, Carlos Zevez.'

CHAPTER 22

'Dad.'

'Yes Tom.'

'I want to stay and help but there's something I need to do first.'

'What's that?'

'I want to go back to Madrid. I've got some unfinished business, a girl I met. I wasn't good with her and I want to make things right.'

'A girl? What, not just any girl?'

'No, she was special.'

'Someone you want to build a lasting, meaningful relationship with?'

'Well, yes, if she'll have me. I didn't realise it at the time, how special she was, but I realise it now. I just hope I'm not too late.'

'Look, you're nearly eighteen. You must make up your own mind about these things, but I'm glad you're taking responsibility and growing up.'

Ralph felt his head swim and he staggered a little.

'Are you all right, Dad?'

'Yes, just a bit tired. Don't you bother about me.' Ralph looked up the hill; Jane was on the path walking towards him. 'There's your mother, I'll see you later.'

'Thanks Dad, and Dad… thanks for being you. Always taking on so much, you know.'

Ralph patted Tom on the back and smiled weakly at him. 'You're a good boy and you'll be a fine man one day.'

Tom smiled back. Ralph carried on up the path but for some reason each step seemed an effort. Jane reached him.

'Ralph, why are you walking away? Carlos is about to give a speech, don't you think you should be there?'

'I don't feel well, suddenly.' His breath came in short sharp bursts.

'You don't look well, so pale, my Ralph.' She put her hand on his arm. 'And so hot.' Now her hand was on his forehead. 'Let me walk you home.'

He saw the love and concern in her face, though his sight was blurring. He wasn't sure if it was the smoky light of the coming evening, a hill fog or his own watery eyes.

'I want to stay but... but I think I should find somewhere quiet and rest.'

'Not think, you must. Here.' She grabbed his hand and tenderly led him along the gravel path. Her long plait swished behind her.

'No, you stay. I'll walk through the wood, the cool trees,' said Ralph.

'I don't want to leave you.'

'Please, you, at least, must hear Carlos' speech.'

She studied him for some moments.

'As you like. Take care.'

Ralph walked on a little then stopped and turned around. He saw that she was still standing there, watching him. He took the path snaking through the coniferous trees standing tall and stately like pillars. He could taste the tangy pine resin at the back of his throat. He shivered suddenly. The backs of his hands looked red, inflamed. There was a hot itchy feeling behind his eyes and a pain developing at the top of his head. As he stumbled on he thought he heard the stream below, but then maybe he didn't, there was some other sort of noise, a noise in his head, the sound of a thousand men and women shouting in pain, a burden almost too much to bear, yes too much. He had a strange, strange feeling of premonition as if this were the end of something. Something final. Then a new sound, a voice. 'Help, help brother.' The voice was thin, with a hint of a refined English accent. Looking ahead through a blur of watery eyes he saw

190

a small wood-panelled hut locked across with a horizontal wooden bar.

'Who's there?' said Ralph.

'Brother, brother, I am locked in, it is terrible accident. Please help me out.'

Using all his strength Ralph removed the wooden bar and the door creaked as he opened it. There, standing in a bloodstained robe and black head wrap was a man with his hands behind his back.

'What's your name?' asked Ralph.

'I am Stefan, a mystic, a friend. Please remove these ties from my wrists.'

Boldly, the man took two paces towards him, his determined eyes fixed on Ralph like two beacons. A bubble of reason flew through Ralph's mind and using all his strength he quickly pushed the man back into the hut. Close to him now, there was a metallic stench of dried blood. The man pushed his head hard against Ralph's chest, Ralph shouted out in pain, lost his balance and stumbled backwards. As the man dodged away Ralph grabbed the robe and the man fell on him; they both went backwards, down, down the hill rolling, rolling. He felt his arms, legs, chest being beaten against dead branches, rocks, stones, as everything went spinning, and heard the groans of the other man, close, too close. Dust and grit were in his eyes. The world flashed by at breakneck speed. Splash, they were in the water, he was being pushed, pulled, driven by nature's force. The waterfall, the waterfall, he thought, I must get out, GET OUT, but there were voices in his head and as he felt himself go over the edge he floated, floated down, and he heard the subdued sound of a soothing chant, soft melodious voices, calling, calling.

Later they found them downstream, Ralph and Malik, in a lifeless embrace like brothers.

CHAPTER 23

Carlos accepted the megaphone from Jalal Kowi, frowned, turned and looked into Sofia's eyes.

'This is another surprise. I've nothing prepared: I don't know what to say.'

A woman near the front shouted, 'Carlos, Carlos.'

Carlos looked out at the vast crowd, men, women, children, some carrying flowers, some waving Hanzzas and Lentas, many with weary battle-worn faces and dishevelled clothes. All looked towards him expectantly. From somewhere in the crowd a loud voice shouted, 'Carlos, talk to us.'

Carlos looked towards Sofia again.

'Speak from within, from your core,' said Sofia gently, patting her hand over her own heart, 'and trust.'

The crowd began chanting 'Carlos' and stamping their feet. As Carlos lifted the megaphone the crowd cheered.

'We have won a battle, but the real battle is not about domination. The battle is about truth over falsehood, expansion over limitation, freedom over enslavement. What have we won? We have won the chance to live differently on our battered planet, to live as one family with tolerance and respect, for surely, if we don't, that will mean the end of humanity. All of us gathered here today have the opportunity to learn from the mistakes of the past and to band together to forge a new society.'

Carlos paused, the children and a few people at the front sat on the ground. The crowd quietened.

'When India gained its independence in 1947 Nehru said, "A moment comes, which comes but rarely in history, when we step out from the old to the new, when an age ends." Today our human family has stopped fighting. What an opportunity this is. This is our moment!'

More people sat down. People quietly joined and stood at the back and around the sides. Carlos felt his mouth go dry and paused, letting the megaphone fall to his side. Sofia thrust a mug of water into his hand and he took a long gulp.

'You're doing well, carry on,' she said. Her face was beaming, her eyes bright and clear. Carlos lifted the megaphone once again.

'We are already in a place where we can rebuild our lives and live differently. The way I'm suggesting is so radically new you may not believe it possible, but we need to try. I don't foresee us rebuilding a new order based on either the ruthless logic of capitalism or the oppression of communism or anything in between. Both of these have been tried and failed. Previous democratic models have also always failed because the goals of their leaders have been short term. We can't think short term any more. Our goals must be long term if we are to survive, in tune with the cycles of nature. Einstein once warned us that "technological progress is like an axe in the hands of a pathological criminal." How right he was.'

Someone shouted, 'Yes!' The crowd chanted 'Carlos, Carlos!'

'Look at them, they love it, they're transfixed,' said Sofia. 'More water?'

Carlos took another gulp. He noticed out of the corner of his eye a group of people dressed in white standing on the shore of the lake building a funeral pyre on a wooden raft. He recognised Isabella's willowy figure and floating gown, and Sunnido's orange robe among the sea of white. Carlos lowered the megaphone and watched for a few moments.

'Don't be distracted, you're doing well,' said Sofia urgently.

'I stand on the shoulders of giants,' said Carlos. 'Of men who had transcendental insight, who were prepared to go counterculture and show us the way. Like the great man

Annando, who spent most of his life helping us to realise our spiritual selves. There is no greater gift that one man or woman can give another than knowledge of the self.' He paused for a moment. 'But I am not your Guru, I don't want to trap anybody: like Krishnamurti, my mission, sprung upon me today, is to set men and women absolutely, unconditionally free.' Exhausted, Carlos loosened his grip on the megaphone and dropped it by his side.

Carlos looked over at Sofia who had tears pouring down her face as did Jalal Kowi, standing next to her. Sofia wrapped her arms around him. 'Well said,' she whispered in his ear. When Sofia stepped back, Jalal Kowi strode forward and clasped him in a strong embrace.

'Yes, well said, my brother,' said Jalal Kowi, as he released his grip.

Erin took both of Carlos' hands in hers. Her eyes were brimming with tears.

'There is *so* much to be done,' she said. 'But we're off to a good start. Well done.'

'Thank you,' said Carlos. 'Yes, much to be done. And first we must say farewell to Annando.'

Erin and Carlos walked slowly over to where Tom stood, his arm protectively around Jane as they watched the funeral preparations. It struck Erin that Tom looked different somehow. No longer a lanky, restless youth. He seemed taller, stronger, more focused. He had an air of calmness about him. A few metres away, Maurice was busy recording the proceedings. Erin smiled. Once a geek, always a geek. He'll never change, she thought, but this will be a brilliant recording. No, never say never, change is the only certainty. Maybe he will surprise us.

'Erin?' She turned. It was Stefano. 'You were right before, you know, on the battlefield. I have a lot to learn. Can you… can you help me? Please?'

Erin gave him quick hug. 'Of course, if I can. We are all on this path, learning together.' He's broken through his inertia, she thought with satisfaction. He's on his way at last.

'Here he comes now,' said Carlos. Erin looked in the direction Carlos was pointing. Annando's body, resting high on a litter, was being slowly carried down the hill. She swallowed hard and felt a lump in her throat. Tears brimmed in her eyes. A hand slipped into hers, its grip warm and reassuring. She glanced up and as she looked into Raphael's face she saw the love in his eyes. Wordlessly she laid her head on his shoulder.

As the litter carrying Annando passed by Carlos stepped forward and joined the little procession. He walked at the back, head bowed. When the group reached the lakeside he helped to lift Annando reverently on to the funeral pyre. Colourful flowers were placed all around the body. Eventually, after much solemn chanting and bowing, Sunnido set the base of the pyre alight. The waves rippled softly on the shore as the tall raft, laden with wood, was pushed out on to the water. Grey smoke billowed lightly from below and floated upwards in straight streams in the still air. The fire whistled and sucked and the small bright flame grew into a furious blaze shining like a beacon as the raft slowly drifted away on the deep dark water. The surface of the lake rippled gently in its wake. Looking round Erin saw the crowd was absolutely still.

Jalal Kowi stood next to Sofia and put his arm around her shoulder. She glanced and smiled at him through her tears. They and the rest of the crowd watched as the bright flames died and extinguished themselves; the pyre was reduced to smouldering ashes. The raft, blackened by the fire, floated slowly out of view. A great plume of smoke danced and billowed high up on soft currents of air. The birds called softly to each other; to Erin their songs sounded like a sad lament as if even *they* knew they had just witnessed the passing of a great being. It was a moment of deep and powerful silence. It was a moment of shared sorrow but also of transition and hope; the end of one cycle and the beginning of another.

Alex Rushton has lived in Surrey since 1992. She has worked in Human Resources, Design Research and as a therapist and counsellor. Alex has been writing non-fiction for many years. This is her first novel and is part of a trilogy. The next title to be published will be *The Asymmetric Man*.